COURTING ELIZA

BRIDES OF SOMERSET BOOK TWO

KAREN LYNNE

Courting Eliza

Brides of Somerset Book Two

OTHER BOOKS BY KAREN LYNNE

Brides of Somerset Series

Heirs of Berkshire Series

Join my reader's group and enjoy updates for new books and little bits of tidbits on 19th-century history.

CHAPTER ONE

*E*liza Grant sat curled on the window seat as the crisp scent of late summer drifted in with the soft breeze, ruffling her hair. She had just finished reading her latest letter from Aunt Helena when her father, Owen Grant, entered the morning room of the vicarage, a bundle of papers clutched in his hand.

"Is that a letter from Helena? What news does she have for us?" her father inquired.

"The usual, Father. She wants me to come to Bristol." Eliza let the letter drop to the seat beside her.

"Ah, well, you know how I feel, Lizzie dear," the vicar replied as he peered over his spectacles before returning his attention to his papers.

Eliza watched her father retreat to his office and sighed. Only her family called her Lizzie. She would turn three and twenty this summer, and her Aunt Helena had been trying to entice her to come to Bristol for the

past few summers for a season in Bath. Helena was
married to Mr. Donovan Notley, a shipping merchant.
With only sons, her aunt was anxious to present the
motherless Eliza and her sister Joanne with a
coming out.

It wasn't that she didn't want to visit Aunt Helena,
for her aunt doted on both her sister and her. It was just
that her heart lay here, in Somerset County, with a
certain gentleman, and if there were any chance it would
be reciprocated, well, she didn't want to go off to Bristol
while she still had hope. Only she knew of these tender
feelings in her heart of course, and Eliza was careful to
keep it hidden, but if she didn't take action soon, she
might as well go off to Bristol.

"Lizzie, I need your help with my packing. I just do
not know what to bring," Joanne complained, entering
the parlor. "I do not even want to go to this party. Why
can I not stay here with Papa? You know how I hate a
crowd."

Eliza rose and wrapped her arm through her sister's
as they returned to Joanne's bedchamber where dresses
and underclothing had been strung across the bed.

"I promise this house party will be entertaining,
besides, you need to come and mingle with people. For
next year you will be of age to have a Season in Bath
with Aunt Helena. If you don't put yourself out in
society, how will you be comfortable enough to have a
Season? Or to meet your future husband?"

Her sister blushed. "Oh, Lizzie, who would want to marry me?"

"Why, dear, you are so pretty, who would not want to marry you? Your temperament is sweet. Many a gentleman will be attending you, but only if you are there to be seen. Besides, I need you there with me," Eliza reassured her. "Father will be fine here at the vicarage. It is only for a weekend. You do like Lady Susan?"

"Yes, she is very kind to me, even though she is your particular friend." Joanne's bottom lip extended just a bit.

"As Abby and I have helped Lady Susan plan this party, we have included your friends so you will be comfortable. Even the children will be present. It's for friends and family, very informal. Susan assures me your friends have all accepted. You would not want to disappoint them. I promise you shall enjoy this weekend immensely."

Her sister relaxed and began packing as Eliza helped her choose her dresses. Eliza was six years older than her sister and had taken care of her since their mother died. Joanne had been a shy child but was slowly growing out of it with Eliza's encouragement.

Eliza's friend, Susan Hamilton, had just married James, the dashing Earl of Malmesbury, in the spring a few months earlier. Eliza had stood up for Susan while her father performed the ceremony in the chapel. Now

that summer was over, and the harvest in, a house party
had been planned to celebrate with the new couple.

Lady Abigale Phelips and her brother William were
their neighbors as well as friends. The four of them had
grown up together. Susan had been so happy since her
marriage to James, and Eliza was looking forward to
spending time with them. Abby and William were
coming in the morning to give them a ride to Bowood
House.

Eliza ordered the trunks brought down to the front hall
where they would be taken ahead by wagon, making
sure all was ready before she joined her family in the
morning room.

"Now Joanne, dear, do not worry for me. I shall be
fine. I have my sermons to prepare and visits to make.
Mrs. Baker takes care of our meals, and I shall find
plenty to keep me busy." her father assured her sister.

He brightened. "Lizzie, dear. Do you have
everything ready for your visit?"

"Yes, Father. Our trunks are in the hall. Abby and
William will be here shortly. They have arranged for our
luggage to be taken to Bowood House." Eliza glanced at
her sister, who was busy pushing a biscuit around her
plate.

"I will see you both in a few days." The vicar rose
and gathered the sheaves of paper he regularly carried

around, as he was continually working on the next Sabbath's sermon.

Eliza's family had been part of Montacute since she could remember. Sir George Phelips, William and Abby's father, had given her father the living and vicarage when he was young and it provided a good life for their family. After her mother died, her father had provided for their schooling, dance instructors, music teachers. It had been a very proper upbringing to prepare Joanne and her for a good marriage.

"You will be at the dance, won't you, father?" Eliza asked.

"Yes, dear," he replied as he gave Joanne a pat of encouragement before returning to his study.

Eliza sat, reaching for a piece of toast, adding butter before taking a bite. Sipping the chocolate, the maid poured, Eliza heard the clanking of harnesses and the crunch of gravel as a wagon approached. She stood and went to the window; it was the wagon from Montacute arriving to transport their luggage. She would need to help see that everything was loaded.

"Joanne," she called, returning to the morning room. "The wagon has left, and Abby will be arriving soon."

"I am ready, Lizzie," Joanne replied. She stood and followed Eliza into the hallway. "You are such a mother hen," she teased.

"I know. I can't help it. You look lovely." Her sister's light complexion contrasted with her bright blue eyes, fringed with black lashes. She would turn heads in a few years as she budded into womanhood.

"I have already agreed to enjoy myself this weekend," Joanne retorted, scrunching her nose and, she flipping her gloves at her sister. "So, there is no need to flatter." Joanne slid on her gloves as she fell in step with Eliza. "Miss Sophia and I shall have a great time." She glanced Eliza's way. Her eyes danced with merriment.

"Along with Miss Shaw and Miss Hardgrave, I am sure you will," Eliza flung back.

"Now don't you start on about my friends. I like them very much, and we have great fun together. I know you do not like Sophia, but she and I are best friends and she makes me feel at ease." Her fingers squeezed Eliza's arm. Eliza's heart softened at the pleading look in her sisters's eyes.

"I know." Eliza covered Joanne's hand with hers. "If it were not for her mother, Lady Moore, Sophia might be easier to abide." Her eyes twinkled, an infectious grin softening her words.

Joanne giggled. "Now Eliza, we cannot pick our parents."

"No, we cannot," Eliza agreed. Lady Moore was the town gossip, maybe the worst gossip in the whole county. It wouldn't be so bad if Sophia did not parrot her mother so frequently. Sophia Moore had been her sister's friend since they both were young. She had grown into a stunning beauty with dark, flowing hair and long lashes to match, set off with vivid green eyes, and she knew it. Sophia was confident the opposite in every way to her sister's looks and personality. It was surprising they had stayed friends.

"I promise my complaints shall only be between us." Eliza wrapped her arm around her sister's waist before giving her a squeeze. "I promise to tolerate Sophia with the utmost courtesy."

Abby swept into the vicarage with a swirl of pink skirts swishing around her ankles and, a pretty bonnet framing her perfectly oval face, shining with eagerness. "Eliza," she squealed, "I had to practically drag my brother along to be here on time."

"You certainly did not," William complained as he followed in Abby's wake. "Do not let her fool you, Eliza. We are not late, Abby, as I pointed out not once but several times." As if to confirm his statement, he noted his pocket watch. Snapping it shut, he returned it to his waistcoat pocket with a satisfied nod to his sister.

Abby fluttered her hand at William with impatience. "It is of no consequence, for we are here now." She rushed forward to greet Eliza.

Eliza caught the faint glint of humor in William's startling blue eyes as she peered over his sister's shoulder. A wisp of toffee-colored hair fell across his brow, making her heart skip a beat. His eyebrows rose in amusement at Abby's excited prattle.

"I am glad you are here, and I daresay you are on time, Abby," Eliza reassured her. "The wagon you sent has come and gone, so we may be on our way."

"You see, Abby, all is well." William tweaked his sister's cheek as she walked by.

"William, do not provoke me so," Abby complained, swatting at his hand playfully as they all proceeded out to the waiting carriage.

William graciously helped Joanne into the carriage before turning and extending his hand to her. Eliza caught a whiff of his scent, a mixture of spice, distinctly male. His grip was firm and steady, sending warmth throughout her. Eliza's heart fluttered just as it did every time William was near. She let go quickly, taking a seat beside Joanne. Abby followed with William sitting next to his sister, facing her.

"I never provoke, dear sister," William stated, looking to Eliza for confirmation. His mouth turned down, pretending offense.

"I would say you do not provoke on purpose," Eliza ventured, "but you are a terrible tease, William, and have been since we were children. Sometimes I think you do not know when to stop. Abby is no longer a child."

"Yes," Abby agreed, "Eliza is right. I think you only find joy when you're causing me vexation. You never take anything serious." Abby adjusted her skirt. "You are lucky you have no brother, Eliza."

William heartily protested, but all Eliza saw was the

same mischievous turn of his mouth, never serious, full of jokes, which she enjoyed when they were younger. But she longed for a more mature version of himself now that he was back from his studies.

"As you wish, dear sister. I shall endeavor to keep quiet." William casually leaned against the carriage. He lifted a leg across his knee, tipped his hat over his brow, and closed his eyes, cushioning his head on the velvet curtain covering the window.

"I have been so excited about this party, as the summer has been so dull after the Season," Abby exclaimed to Eliza. "So warm and muggy. I am glad it begins to cool." Eliza agreed. The summer had been warm, and she loved the coolness of fall. Abby continued to talk about her excitement over her next Season in London.

Eliza stole a glance at William as he slumbered, or pretended to. She suspected he was listening to every word as his sister continued her chatter. He had grown while away, leaving behind his boyish looks. His coat and pantaloons fit nicely over his firm muscled body. She turned to the window, pulling the curtains back, and peered out where the view was safer for her thoughts. Would he ever think of her as something more than a friend?

CHAPTER TWO

*B*owood House, home of Lord and Lady Malmesbury, appeared in the distance as the carriage emerged from the woods. The estate sat on four thousand acres of pristine land. One could not help but be impressed as the morning sun shone in the cloudless sky, giving the scene a soft glow. It made a beautiful picture, Eliza thought, keeping her mind turned to safer images. The carriage wheels clicked against the cobblestones as they entered the courtyard.

A line of servants dressed in crisp uniforms waited to receive guests. Eliza could see Susan at the top of the stairs as the carriage pulled to a stop. Footmen quickly lowered the steps and opened the door.

Susan reached out to grasp Eliza's hands. "Eliza, Abby, it seems we are a success, as the party has been well received. Guests will be arriving this afternoon, just before luncheon."

"That is wonderful, my lady." Susan had worried about her acceptance in the community after marrying the earl. Susan had been well-liked before she married James, Eliza reminded her, and the rest of the community well... they — would come to love and respect her friend as time passed.

"Eliza, we have no need to be formal among friends." Susan wrinkled her nose. "Please call me Susan, at least here in my home."

"Yes, Susan." She would need to adjust to her new status now that she was a countess, Eliza thought.

"I hear 'my lady' all day long from the servants," Susan complained. "I do not need to hear it from my friends. James assures me it is quite acceptable while we are at home."

Susan walked over to Joanne, taking her by the arm. "Joanne, I have arranged for you to be in rooms near your friends, Miss Moore, and Miss Shaw. Mrs. Oakley, the housekeeper, will show you to your room," Susan nodded to the housekeeper. "A maid has been assigned to help you while you are here. Do not hesitate to ask for anything you may need." A young miss stepped forward on Susan's announcement and curtsied to her sister.

Joanne followed behind the housekeeper, then turning, she mouthed silently to Eliza, "Thank you."

"Susan, that was very good of you to put the girls by each other."

The new countess linked her arms with Abby and

Eliza's, guiding them up the impressive flight of stairs, that curved along the wall. Plush carpet cushioned their steps. "The best part is, James' mother, the Dowager Countess, handled Lady Moore famously, convincing her she need not spend the weekend here at Bowood House with her daughter, but that she could come each day by carriage."

Eliza relaxed. "That is good news, indeed."

"Now," Susan explained, "I have you both in the family wing close to me. Better for us to gossip in the evenings, amongst ourselves."

They were led down a wide hall. Carpet runners quieted their footsteps on the stone tiles worn from generations of use. Large windows looked out onto the inner courtyard.

"Here we are." Susan stopped at a white-paneled door. "Abby, this is your room. I have been informed your maid has arrived and is here already unpacking."

"Eliza, your room is the next one here. I have assigned a maid to take care of you throughout your stay, as well." Susan smiled. "Now you both may get settled. A luncheon for the ladies will be served at one o'clock. Do not hesitate to ask any servant for directions. This house is rather large. I have already been lost several times," Susan admitted retreating back down the hall.

Abby took hold of Eliza's hands and gave a little squeal of delight. "This weekend will be so amusing. I love that we are all here together," Abby cooed.

"I shall knock when I am ready to go downstairs," Eliza informed Abby, before entering her room.

Eliza's bed-chamber was delightful. Two large windows, framed with floral drapes and window seats — a cozy place to read, she thought—looked out onto the back gardens. Eliza could just see a lake through a copse of trees.

A knock sounded at the door before a young maid entered, giving Eliza a quick curtsy. "I am to look after you while you are visiting, miss." She looked toward Eliza, her eyes not making contact.

The maid appeared quite young, with a pleasing countenance. Probably one of the lower maids, pulled from her duties to help with the guests. "That would be wonderful. What is your name?"

"Sally, miss."

"Thank you, Sally, I am to get ready for luncheon soon." Eliza stepped aside as Sally moved to unpack. "I will be wearing the blue muslin."

"Yes, miss."

Eliza's mind turned to William, and how well he looked. He had slipped away shortly after they entered the house. Eliza determined to find out his true feelings for her. If there was any hope.

She and Abby entered the salon where a luncheon of cold meats, assortments of cheese, bread and sweetmeats had been set up on the buffet. A soft hum filled the room as ladies talked.

Susan greeted Eliza wrapping her arm around her waist.

"You have a good group here, and you were worried," Eliza whispered.

"Yes, well, it is my first entertainment as the new countess. James and his mother have been very supportive. The dowager looked over our guest list and, pointed out important people I had missed," Susan explained. "There are so many rules a countess must observe. Thank heavens for the dowager's help."

"You will do well, Susan," Eliza encouraged her. "I have never seen you back down from a challenge yet."

Eliza knew William would be married someday. Would his Aunt Lucy be as gracious to a new bride at Montacute? She had hoped it would be her, but William had not shown any interest in her beyond a boyhood friend which they could no longer be now that they were grown.

Joanne and her friends were at a table by the terrace windows. "Susan, as much as I dislike Miss Sophia, I am pleased that you were able to arrange her visit."

Susan laughed. "Yes, considering how much Lady Moore irritates his Lordship. The Dowager has promised to keep her busy and out of James' way."

"It is only because Lady Moore had set her cap for her daughter to marry James. You left her disappointed. I am curious to see how the dowager will accomplish that feat." Eliza giggled.

"Poor Lady Moore. James would never have chosen Sophia; she is much too young."

Eliza could think of other reasons, but she held her tongue. A lady didn't gossip.

Eliza enjoyed the rest of the afternoon spending time with the ladies. Susan had informed her that James had the gentlemen riding about the countryside, doing whatever gentlemen did; she had no clue. William's father, Sir George, spent most of his time in London, serving in Parliament. Her own father was always home, puttering around the vicarage, planning his sermons and visiting his parishioners. Although her father could have hired a curate to handle the ministering of his flock, he preferred to handle the work himself.

Most of the ladies retired to their rooms after luncheon to rest before dinner. Susan offered a tour of Bowood House, for any lady that wished. Eliza was most impressed with the library. She would come back later and explore the books. The tour was beneficial, for she could see that Susan was right. One could indeed get lost in the large house.

Eliza was restless and decided to explore the library further, borrow a book or two that she might read in her room. Slipping into the hallway she made her way back to the main house. Asking for directions only once before standing outside a set of wide double doors. She tested the doorknob, and it turned easily on well-oiled hinges. Peeking around the door to check for occupants, the room appeared empty. Eliza slipped into the vast space filled with heavily laden shelves. A ladder on wheels ran along rungs, enabling anyone to reach the top shelves.

An impressive balcony ran along one end of the room, accessible by a beautiful stairwell running along the wall. More bookshelves soared all the way to the top of the fifteen-foot ceiling. Her heart swelled as she climbed towards the balcony. Eliza's fingers tickled the row of books, the pungent smell of leather assaulting her senses. She was in heaven. Nothing like a good book to put her to rights.

Her father's library contained books on theology. Eliza treasured her small collection of novels gathered throughout the years. She remembered how William had teased her whenever he found her absorbed in a new book. She ran her fingers along the hard leather bindings, pulling a book from the shelf. A sound from below startled her as she swung around, holding the book to her chest. Eliza met the eyes of a stranger, looking at her from below.

"Sir, you startled me," Eliza exclaimed before realizing her slip at addressing a gentleman to whom she had not been introduced. Blushing, her hand flew to her lips.

Penetrating eyes watched her. In a split second, before the stranger spoke, she assessed him as having a serious nature, being conservatively well-dressed with sideburns tickling his chin. He must be at least ten years her senior.

"I am sorry I startled you, miss." He looked around, his arms indicating the empty room. "As there is no one to introduce us, may I?"

Eliza gave a slight nod.

"Sir Martin Wycliff, at your service, miss." He gave her a bow. "It appears you were looking for a book."

Eliza relaxed her grip on the book. "Miss Grant, Sir Martin." A slight smile played at her lips. "I was restless and thought to find a novel to read before dinner. I apologize if I disturbed you. I did not notice anyone here when I entered."

"Oh no, Miss Grant, you have not disturbed me." He tucked a bundle of papers into his coat pocket.

"I will leave you in peace and hope we are introduced more formally at dinner." His eyes danced as he held his finger to his lips. "I will tell no one we have met," Sir Martin replied as he closed the door behind him.

Eliza slipped the book back on the shelf. What a strange gentleman, he must be here for the party. Finding a novel, she tucked it under her arm and returned to her bed-chamber. The late afternoon sun had warmed the room as it streamed through the windows. The maid had put a vase of late summer flowers on the small table by her bed, further cheering up the already bright room. Settling on a window seat, Eliza began to read.

CHAPTER THREE

*W*illiam left the ladies in the hallway and followed the butler to his room. His valet had arrived earlier; his luggage was unpacked, riding clothes ready. The gentleman guests would be riding out at one o'clock to tour the estate.

William had been running his father's estate, Montacute, throughout the summer. He had been trained up while young to manage the country house. It had been a good harvest, but now he was ready to enjoy the company of his neighbors.

He had looked forward to this house party. Susan and James had promised Abby this celebration at the end of the summer as she was disappointed in not being able to attend their spring wedding. His father insisted she stay and finish out the Season in London.

Abby had prodded him this morning, eager to get here, enjoying their playful banter. It had been a long time since they had been together. After his schooling, he spent a few years traveling to different estates, observing the different techniques they each applied. He had conferred with James, and they had implemented some things he had learned with excellent results. William looked forward to the ride today. He brought his own mount, although James had started to replenish his stables after his marriage to Susan, acquiring some exceptional bloodlines at Tattersalls.

Abby had grown into a young lady while he had been away, though she was still impulsive with an exuberant personality. He could still rile her with his teasing. Eliza had grown into a beauty as well, quieter and more serious than Abby, but he found he could still tease a smile out of her. Eliza was right of course, the young girls he had grown up and romped through the hills with, were gone.

William could see James as he approached the stables, organizing the gentlemen as they picked their mounts. Stable dogs spun around his legs, wagging their tails, excited to get their master's attention. William inhaled the scent of freshly scattered straw in the fresh morning air.

"William, you have arrived." James approached, giving him the usual slap on the back as they greeted each other.

"Yes." William chuckled. "Abby was very insistent. I get moving this morning. I have left her and the Grant sisters in the care of your wife."

William retrieved his horse from a stable hand. Other gentlemen had chosen their mounts.

"I thought you would enjoy a tour of the estate today, then off to town for a bite to eat at the tavern. There shall be grouse hunting tomorrow morning. Susan has planned a dinner at six," James explained, "so we had better get moving." He chuckled. "Cook would have my head if we were late."

"William." Captain Charles Rutley approached, a gentleman following behind. "I would like you to meet a friend, Sir Martin Wycliff from Bristol."

"Sir Martin, this is William Phelips," Charles introduced them.

"Bristol, you say? That is a busy port town, is it not?" William nodded, meeting Sir Martin's penetrating brown eyes. His whiskers made him appear older.

"Yes, it is." He offered his hand, giving William a firm handshake.

"Sir Martin has an investment opportunity. I thought you could join us, along with James to discuss it after dinner," the captain informed him.

William nodded his consent. He was always looking for some sound investments. If this, Sir Martin was trustworthy.

"Well, it would do no harm to listen," William agreed.

∼

The gentlemen retired to change after their ride. James informed his guests the time was theirs before dinner.

"We have billiards or cards in the game room and plenty to read in the library, of course," James explained. "If you get lost," he chuckled, "just ask a footman. They will get you back on course."

William suspected James meant to spend the short interlude before dinner with his wife.

William's valet waited to help him wash and dress. He mused over the change in Susan since her marriage. James was not ashamed to show his affection for his new wife, which was unusual for aristocratic families.

He decided he wanted that for himself, although the thoughts of marriage—well, he was still young. He had escorted his sister Abby to her first Season, along with his aunt Lucy, this past spring and soon grew tired of the constant round of visits and parties. He found the country more to his liking, unlike his peers who wiled the time away in London gambling and socializing. He found more satisfaction in working the estate.

William left his chambers in search of some company after dressing. The game room was quiet. A few gentlemen played billiards while a couple of gentlemen bent over a chessboard. William turned. Preferring the outdoors, a walk in the gardens would be more to his liking

Rounding a bend in the garden path, he recognized a familiar silhouette sitting on a stone bench under the shade of a tree, her bonnet thrown to the side. How many times had he caught Eliza in this very pose, immersed in a novel, captivated by its contents, oblivious to the world around her? Soft brown curls fell over her pink cheeks. Her figure filled out the green dress in all the right places. He still couldn't believe the change. She had grown into a beauty.

He approached, quietly leaving the path to sneak up from behind her. Something tightened in his chest, but he shook off the feeling before he leaned over her left shoulder and snatched the book from her grasp.

She squealed, turning her wide green eyes to him. Her hand flew to her lips. "William, you scared me." Eliza's eyes flashed.

"I couldn't resist," he admitted. "How many times have I caught you reading?"

"Too many, I assure you," she remarked. William noticed the annoyance in her voice. She looked around before quickly reaching for her book.

William turned, raising it just out of her reach and swung around the tree. She followed, trying to snatch it from his hands. She stopped suddenly, her hands on her hips. Her soft curls falling from her pins made her look adorable. "William, please, we are no longer children playing silly games," she retorted as she brushed the strands aside.

Her eyes flashed like fire. My, she was pretty he thought as he stepped towards her, offering her the book.

She reached forward to retrieve her book. William

didn't know why, but he raised the book once again just out of her reach. This time she stumbled, and he reached out, wrapping his arm around her waist to catch her, surprised at how good she smelled. Her shocked, wide eyes lifted to his as William held her close. He scanned her face and settled his eyes on her lips. They were so close, if he just leaned in, he could taste them.

"Excuse me," William whispered.

Eliza emitted a soft cry before quickly pulling away, grabbing the book from his hand before retreating toward the path. Turning she bumped into a surprised Sir Martin, who reached out to steady her. Eliza stepped back, rose coloring her cheeks, she adjusted her skirts.

"Sir Martin," William spoke as he approached Eliza from behind.

Sir Martin coughed. "I apologize, I did not mean to interrupt anything." He stepped back as if to leave.

"Wait," Eliza sputtered, turning pleading eyes on William.

"Sir Martin, no, it is not what you think. May I introduce Miss Grant? Miss Grant, this is Sir Martin Wycliff, a friend of Captain Rutley's. He is visiting us from Bristol."

Eliza gave Sir Martin a small nod. "Nice to meet you, Sir Martin," her cheeks still pink.

William felt terrible that he had embarrassed her, and now, Sir Martin clearly thought he was interrupting something between them. She was right; they were no longer children. Guilt assailed him. Habits were hard to break. Eliza clearly deserved more respect, especially from him.

"Miss Grant and I are childhood friends," William explained. "I have a habit of plaguing her with my teasing."

Eliza threw William a look, her eyes shining. "I was just returning to the house, Sir Martin."

"Perhaps I can escort you. I believe dinner is to be served soon." Sir Martin offered his arm.

"Thank you, Sir Martin. That would be lovely." Eliza took his arm, walking with him in the direction of the house.

William stood, watching their backs. Turning her head, Eliza threw him a brief look, a scowl really, over her shoulder before they turned and were out of sight. He was perplexed by the new feelings he felt as he had held Eliza in his arms. William had almost kissed her. What was he thinking? He clearly did not like Sir Martin escorting her to the house.

Drat the man.

Eliza's bonnet sat on the stone bench where she left it. Walking over, he scooped it up, rubbing his fingers along the silk ribbons. He would return it when she calmed down.

Eliza's chest pounded as they walked through the garden. She willed it to calm. Had William almost kissed her? In the presence of Sir Martin, no less. What must he think of her? She gave Sir Martin a sidelong glance. Better to not mention anything, pretend all was normal. Her face warmed. The sound of birds chirping in the hedges filled the silence. The sunlight waned, creating a soft glow through the bushes. Soon it would be dark.

"Sir Martin," she lifted her eyes and smiled, "William mentioned you were from Bristol." She spoke in her most engaging voice.

"Yes, it is my home, although I do business in London, Bath, and other cities. Do you know the city?"

"I have not been for several years, but I often visited my aunt and uncle who reside there."

They had reached the house, entering through the terrace doors. A drone of voices could be heard. Eliza thanked Sir Martin for his attendance before quickly joining the rest of the company in the parlor, cutting short their conversation.

Eliza's ire raised at William's teasing. How dare he compromise her in front of Sir Martin! Wait, was she truly compromised? Well, anyway, she was extremely peeved at him none-the-less. At least Sir Martin showed some respect. William could take a lesson from the gentleman.

∼

William entered Bowood House, avoiding the parlor where the sound of voices and laughter could be heard. Pausing at the game room door he heard the cracking of billiard balls before entering. The smell of tobacco engulfed the room; he noted Sir Martin wasn't present.

James and Charles partnered at the billiard table. James aimed his cue stick in while the captain watched, leaning on the edge of the table. William tossed Eliza's bonnet on a nearby chair, and he ran his fingers through a tuft of his bronze hair. His chest felt tight. Why was he feeling so guilty? It wasn't Eliza's fiery eyes blazing at him while he held her close; he liked that feeling. It was the embarrassment he'd seen on her face as she ran into Sir Martin.

"Dinner is served, my lord," the butler announced.

"Ah, gentlemen, let us remove to the dining room," James said.

As gentlemen filed past William, Charles stopped and clapped him on the shoulder. "What is it that has you so sullen, my man?"

William eyed the bonnet he'd dropped on the chair. He waited for the room to clear. "Miss Grant, Eliza, I may have damaged our friendship." He muttered, "I have always teased her, but today I fear I have embarrassed her in front of Sir Martin, a stranger, no less." William sighed as he walked over to the hearth and sunk into a rich leather chair. Dropping his head into his hands, he rubbed his temples.

Charles followed, sitting in the chair facing William. "Embarrassed her? Are you sure she was embarrassed?"

William sat, rubbing his forehead. "Sir Martin came upon us as Eliza was chasing me around a tree."

Charles chuckled, rubbing his chin. "Chasing you around a tree, I see. Not very proper considering your age."

William watched him under hooded eyes. "I had taken the book she was reading, and Eliza was trying to get it back." William did not dare mention the accidental embrace and the feelings it sparked.

A footman entered and began lighting the lamps. William watched him silently making his way around the room, touching a torch to the lamps, one by one. Charles followed his eyes, waiting until they were alone again.

"I see," Charles shook his head as the footman retreated to the hall. "Yes, you are right. I think she was not comfortable. What lady would be?"

"I was hoping to return her bonnet and apologize." William looked over to the chair. "I would hate to lose our friendship." The thought of never being able to joke with Eliza again depressed him.

"Well, then," Charles replied, "I suggest you send her a note with the return of her bonnet. Send it to her room where she will find it when she retires for the night. Do it up right," Charles continued. "Women love it when a man admits he was wrong."

William brightened. "Yes, a note. I will have it

delivered to her room, as you say." He stood, retrieving some writing paper from a nearby desk. "I am not above groveling." His brow clouded.

"What is the matter now?" Charles asked.

"I have not a clue what to write. I don't think I have ever written a note of apology."

"Come, I will help. I have written my share of groveling apology letters." Charles chuckled, his voice light.

Together with Charles over the next hour, they composed William's letter.

After the letter had been delivered to the butler with instructions to add a cluster of posies for good measure, both men sank back into the chairs by the hearth.

"Thank you, Charles. I could not have done that on my own. I would have bumbled it and made things worse."

"I understand." Charles stood and poured them a drink, handing one to William. "It's hard to write to the ladies. Even one you've known all your life."

The hum in the parlor subsided as Lady Susan tapped a glass.

"Lord Malmesbury has informed me that dinner is ready," Susan declared to the waiting group. "We are informal here, so please, sit where you please." Susan smiled as James placed her arm in his and led the group to the dining room.

The lamps had been lit, and the table sparkled with the earl's finest setting of china, embossed with the family's crest. Several footmen lined the walls, waiting to serve the guests. Eliza claimed a seat to the right of Susan with James at the head of the long table. The Dowager Countess sat at the other end, surrounded by her confidants. Joanne sat next to Sophia and her friends in the middle of the table. Eliza was delighted to see her sister cheerful in their company. Her sister had appeared to forget her shyness.

"Eliza," Abby whispered as she sat to her left. "Have you seen William?"

"He was in the garden earlier." Eliza glanced down the table. Concerned, she shifted in her chair, and her ire quickly turned to concern an uneasy feeling in her breast.

"I do not see Captain Rutley. They must be together," Abby mused, more to herself than to Eliza.

She thought about the garden. What if she had let William kiss her? Would he have, had she not moved? Did this mean he had feelings for her, other than friendship? Eliza occasionally glanced at the door. William did not show himself. Her heart sank just a little. She hoped he was not mad at her for leaving with Sir Martin.

The meal proceeded with footmen delivering the first course. Susan's cook had done a marvelous job with the meal. The party was starting to be a great success, in more ways than one, Eliza could feel it, remembering the warmth of standing in William's arms.

The clattering of silver brought Eliza back from her thoughts.

"Ladies, we will leave the gentlemen to discuss their business." Susan squeezed James' hand, a gentle smile on her face. "Gentlemen, you may join us when you exhaust your topics of discussion."

The scraping of chairs filled the room as the gentlemen rose, ladies left the dining room a few at a time. Abby and Susan tucked their arms through Eliza's.

"There they are." Abby giggled. "It must have been important for William to miss a meal."

A clock chimed. "I am afraid we have missed dinner." William glanced at the mantel.

"Always glad to help with young love." Charles waved his hand, rising from his chair.

Young love! William was not in love. Eliza was just a friend. But before he could object, Charles had risen. Offering his hand, William let Charles help him to his feet.

"I think we can make it in time for brandy." Charles patted him on the back.

They walked into the dining hall as the ladies were leaving. He glimpsed Eliza through the crowd, speaking with his sister. Calm wafted over him. He would be more attentive; she sparked a protective flame in him. They were both adults now. It was only natural that their relationship would shift and change. It wasn't proper for ladies to be romping around with unmarried gentlemen. He must be more careful with her reputation, just as he would with Abby's.

Gentlemen sat down in their seats as the door closed behind the ladies. William sat flanking James while murmuring voices filled the room. A plate of food appeared before him. A footman poured wine in a clean crystal goblet.

"You didn't think I would let you miss dinner?" James informed him.

"Sir Martin, Rutley tells us you have some investment ideas you want to discuss." James turned to Sir Martin.

"I have told them about Mr. Notley accepting investors for his next voyage to the Americas before spring," Charles explained. "I have not given them any details about the percentages or the cargo." He fingered the stem of his glass.

"Charles and I have been investing in Mr. Notley's shipping business for years. We can attest to his honesty and the success of his business," Sir Martin explained. "Mr. Notley's main business is tobacco and cocoa beans. He is looking for investors for his next shipment, and Charles thought you might be interested."

"This all sounds promising." William pushed his

empty plate away, wiped his mouth, folded his napkin, laid it aside and took a drink of brandy.

"I agree," James replied, "why don't we talk it over in more detail tomorrow after the picnic? Shall we meet in the library?" Three heads nodded agreement. "Gentlemen I believe we have left the ladies waiting long enough." James stood, pushed back his chair, and led the way to the drawing room.

CHAPTER FOUR

*E*liza's attention shifted to the ladies as they gathered in the drawing-room. Abby wandered toward the pianoforte, shuffling through the sheets of music before she picked a piece, and began to play. Eliza joined her on the bench seat and turned the sheet music. Susan walked over and leaned against the wall. "I have informed my husband, that I shall be retiring after an appropriate amount of time," Susan whispered. "Shall we meet at my salon, in say a half an hour?"

"I think that is an excellent idea," Abby agreed with a nod of her head. "We will meet you there prepared for some friendly gossip."

Eliza smiled, nodding her head.

A low murmuring could be heard in the hall as gentlemen came into the drawing-room a few at a time. Susan pulled away from the wall and meandered over to her husband while talking to guests. She leaned and whispered in James' ear. He wrapped his arm gently around her waist as he nuzzled her ear, whispering something that made Susan giggle and nod her head. Susan advanced toward the door as James watched, his eyes never leaving her until she disappeared into the hall.

Eliza felt a wave of envy as she witnessed the tender scene between her friends. Is that how it would be for her? She hoped to find a husband who loved her as much as it appeared, James loved Susan. Eliza drew a breath and dared to sneak a glance at William.

His dark brow furrowed as he concentrated on something Sir Martin discussed. Charles joined their conversation. They must be discussing something important to capture William's attention so thoroughly. Her gaze traveled over his face, admiring his form before tearing her eyes away.

She leaned over to Abby, whispering in her ear. Abby nodded agreement. Eliza left the parlor. Slipping up to her room, she found the young maid asleep in a chair, her embroidery fallen from her hand, draped at her foot. A basket of threads set by the chair. Eliza smiled, reaching to retrieve the material and brushed across Sally's hand. Startled, the maid woke, rubbing sleep from her eyes.

"Oh, miss." She quickly stood. "I waited in case you needed me." She reached for her sewing and gathered her basket, tucking it away before coming to undress Eliza.

"Thank you, Sally."

Eliza picked a dressing gown from the wardrobe and gave Sally her back as she helped her undress, then slipped into her nightgown. She and Joanne always helped each other in the vicarage. Sally's fingers were gentle and unsure as she performed her duties.

"Sally, I am going to visit with Lady Malmesbury in her parlor. You need not wait up for me."

"Yes, miss." Sally bobbed. "A gentleman left a note here miss. If there is nothing else?"

"No, Sally, that will be all."

Eliza reached for the note lying beside her bonnet. William must have returned it. She hadn't realized she'd left it. Eliza opened the note, smiling at his clumsy attempt to apologize. William wanted her to forgive his teasing, that Eliza was right, they were no longer children. He promised to treat her as such. Would she still be his friend and forgive him? She folded the note and tucked it under her bonnet. Of course, she would forgive him. Lifting the small bundle of posies to her nose, she breathed in the fresh scent. She already had.

Eliza knocked softly on Susan's door. It opened a crack. Abby's smiling face greeted her. She lifted her fingers to her lips, letting Eliza slide through the door. Abby pointed to where Susan was sleeping, her feet tucked underneath her gown as she dozed on a rose-patterned sofa opposite two fluffy chairs by the hearth.

"Shall we wake her?"

"No, let her sleep. She will wake soon enough," Abby whispered.

A pot of hot chocolate, surrounded by dainty biscuits, sat on an ornate silver tray on the small table by the sofa. Abby poured a cup before handing it to her. Eliza sipped the warm liquid as she gazed around the intimate parlor.

Two windows draped with the same chintz fabric as the sofa reflected the lamplight. Darkness had fallen, obscuring the view which she suspected faced the gardens. A small oak desk sat behind the sofa against the light paneled walls, a private place for Susan to write her correspondence.

"This room is perfect. Do you think Susan decorated it herself?"

"I should think not. Does Susan even know how to pick fabrics?" Abby replied.

"I can hear you both," Susan complained, as her eyes fluttered open. "No, I did not, the dowager countess had it done for me as a wedding present." Susan stretched as she sat up.

"Well, I just love it. I would spend as much time here as possible," Eliza cooed. "Give me a good book, and I am in heaven." She picked up a biscuit, inhaling the aroma of the chocolate.

"Eliza, give you any book and you would be happy, even under a dead tree." Abby laughed.

Eliza had to agree. She loved to learn, and books

were the best way since she didn't travel much. But someday, she would.

Susan reached for the ivory papers on the table. "I have a program of tomorrow's activities." Susan handed Eliza a sheet. "I thought you would like a peek. They shall be available at breakfast for the guests."

"Eliza, we should paint a landscape. Here, they are to be in watercolors." Abby pointed to the entry on her paper.

"They are to be judged, Abby, and I do not paint well at all." Eliza scanned the program.

"It will be fun, but you may do whatever you wish. I want the guests to relax and enjoy their day. There will be a dance in the evening before the party breaks up after services on Sunday," Susan reassured her.

Eliza pointed to the list. "A picnic, what fun. We will pack our own baskets, and the gentlemen will be obliged to share with us. What a fun activity. How clever Susan. The gentlemen will have to share lunch with us instead of running off to the village."

"I cannot take the credit, but I thought it an enjoyable way to mingle. Each unmarried lady will pack a basket, and the gentleman bachelors will pick a number," said Susan.

"Matching numbers will share a meal. I agree. It is clever." Abby clapped her hands.

"It will all be perfectly random, so the young ladies will not feel slighted. The dowager countess said it really works to promote conversation. By evening when we have our dance, everyone should feel more comfortable," Susan said.

They talked into the late evening. Susan began to wilt as her eyes grew heavy, and she struggled to keep them open. "Abby, I think we need to go to bed and let Susan get her rest," Eliza whispered.

"I will see you in the morning, then. Shall we go for a morning ride before breakfast?" Abby whispered.

"I would like that. Say at six o'clock?"

"Six is perfect." Abby nodded.

"Six, why so early?" Susan complained.

They both laughed. Susan's eyes flickered open.

"You may stay a bed if you wish, Susan, but we like the crisp mornings," Eliza answered.

"Just send us word if you cannot make it in the morning. Then we shan't wait for you." Abby told Susan.

Eliza found Abby dressed and at the stables early the next morning. Eliza had chosen her most beautiful riding habit. You never knew who you would meet, she reasoned as she thought of William. Two mounts were waiting in the stable yard held by a groom.

"Susan wasn't able to join us?" Eliza asked, looking at the two horses. She accepted the reins to the black mare.

"Her maid sent word that she wouldn't be coming."

Abby shrugged. "She wants us to enjoy our ride without her." She reached for the gray mare's reins, leading her to the mounting block. Abby quickly adjusted her skirts as the groom steadied the animal.

Eliza led her mount into the lane. She adjusted her skirts across the pummel before urging the horse into a canter. Abby followed as they turned out into the countryside, a groom following at a distance. Eliza's velvet riding habit had been a good choice. It protected her against the chill of the fall morning.

The two of them crossed into Abby's father's estate lands as they crested the hill. William's family home of Montacute came into view. The estate stretched out over the vast rolling hills. Two riders could be seen coming in their direction.

"I do believe that is William," Abby said as she stopped her horse beside Eliza, her hand shading her eyes. "Come, let's meet them." Abby pushed her mount forward.

James and William greeted the ladies as they rode up alongside them. "We were just heading back to Bowood House. May we escort you?" James asked.

"Yes, it is time we returned," Abby fell in beside James. "Susan declined to join us at such an early hour."

"She has been sleeping in later for the past month," James said.

William moved up beside Eliza as she let James and Abby take the lead. He was quiet, which was unusual for him, so she took pity and spoke first.

"Thank you for returning my bonnet, William. I did not know I left it in the garden." She ducked her head.

"I'm sorry for embarrassing you, Eliza." William slapped his hand against his pants, knocking the dust away. "I meant what I said about treating you like a lady. I hadn't meant to make things awkward between us, I know I need to be careful of your reputation." He lowered his head, adjusting his boot in the stirrup.

"That is good of you, William. Let's see how long it will last," she gave him a smile.

His head shot up, giving her a protesting look, relaxing at her teasing. "You don't think I can," he shot back. "Stop teasing, that is."

Eliza laughed. "I think it is ingrained in your character. It is one of the things I like about you," she admitted. "But I am glad to hear you want to protect my reputation."

"You'll see, I may surprise you," William promised.

"Is my brother provoking you?" Abby called over her shoulder as they neared the stables.

Eliza breathed, "William has declared he will no longer tease, but shall endeavor to treat me like a lady, as we are no longer children. A fact I reminded him of yesterday."

Abby clapped her hands in delight. "I should like to lay a wager on that." She laughed.

"I'm afraid the odds are in our favor," Eliza declared with a chuckle.

"I see that neither of you has confidence in me."

William threw his leg over the saddle and dismounted, handing the groom his reins.

Approaching Eliza, he took her reins as they slid from her grip. "May I help you dismount?" he asked.

She gave him a shy smile. "You may, William."

Eliza untangled her skirt from the pommel as he advanced. William reached his hands to her waist, and she slid to the ground. Shivers pulsed through her at his touch. She let her hands slide from his broad shoulders. They were standing close, his bright blue eyes shining down at her. Eliza would have liked to stay close as William dropped his hands from her waist. She inhaled his scent after his long ride. Reluctantly, she stepped away, putting the appropriate distance between them.

Abby stepped beside her and laced her arm in Eliza's. "See you later, William." She smiled at her brother as they returned to the house.

Eliza glanced over her shoulder as they retreated. William gave her a friendly salute before turning his attention back to James.

CHAPTER FIVE

*E*liza changed from her riding habit before making her way to the breakfast room, ready to break her fast. The aroma of bacon in the hall made her stomach churn. The ride this morning had certainly increased her appetite.

A scrumptious buffet had been set up on the large sideboard along the wall. Attendants were keeping the dishes filled and pouring hot drinks. Eliza helped herself to a plate of crumpets, and fresh peaches topped with cream. She found a seat by Susan and Abby. Groups of tables were clustered around the room. Glass pitchers filled with a variety of juices acted as centerpieces, sparkling off the sun coming through the terrace.

Eliza reached for a pitcher and filled her glass. The effect was very cheery, she thought. "Abby and I had an exhilarating ride this morning. We wished you could have joined us. We met James and William on the return home." Eliza folded a napkin across her lap before reaching for a crumpet.

"I have been feeling rather queasy in the mornings, and riding makes it worse," Susan said.

"Queasy? Have you seen a physician?" Eliza asked, spreading jam across her bread.

"A physician!" Susan waved her hand, taking a sip of juice. "I would not trust the local man."

"My maid made me some ginger tea. It passed, and I'm feeling much better now."

Eliza relaxed, still concerned as she took another bite of her crumpet. "James said you have been sleeping later in the mornings."

The sound of baying dogs could be heard in the distance as a cool breeze drifted through the open windows. "The gentlemen were up early," Abby said.

"James took the gentlemen hunting this morning. I think most of the gentlemen wanted an excuse to roam the countryside. Grouse will be an excellent addition to the dinner menu tonight." Susan said, sipping from her cup.

Susan rose from the table and walked to the front of the parlor. The murmurs subsided as the room quieted. "Ladies, we have a luncheon on the lawn planned this afternoon. The gentlemen will be joining us after the hunt this afternoon for a picnic. The cook has set out a wonderful buffet of delights. All the unmarried ladies may pick a basket to fill, which you will share with a gentleman." Susan smiled.

The room filled with excitement as the young ladies whispered amongst themselves.

"We thought it would be a relaxing way for some gentlemen to get to know you better before our country dance tonight." Susan turned her attention to the dowager countess.

The dowager stood but stayed by her table as she continued the instructions. "To make it interesting, each of your baskets will have a number. Ladies, the gentlemen will pick a number with your name, each in turn. The gentleman with your number will share your basket."

The room exploded with a buzz as the young ladies' excited chatter filled the air.

"You may finish with your breakfast before filling your baskets. We have ribbons for you to tie on the handles to identify which is yours," the dowager countess sat back in her seat.

Susan waved her hands to quiet the room. "We have written a program for the activities today. You may pick up one as you leave. Easels with watercolors are set up in the grove of trees for anyone who wants to participate in painting the beautiful prospect. A few gentlemen have been appointed to judge the paintings, and the winner will lead the first quadrille tonight at the dance."

Eliza and Abby finished their meal, then went and picked baskets. "Are you going to come and paint with me?" Abby asked. Moving down the table, she placed various foods into her basket. Eliza did the same, paying little attention to the lunch she was assembling.

"Abby, I don't paint," Eliza reminded her. She had always rushed through her lessons with her music, and art masters. She preferred the out-of-doors and visiting with parishioners, and reading of course.

"Please," Abby begged, "It will be fun."

"Fine," Eliza relented. Finishing their lunch baskets, they wandered through the grove, picking a spot where they liked the view of the landscape. Eliza sat on a stool, adjusting the paper on her easel. She dipped her brush in the tin of water and swirled it through the color blue. Reaching her brush towards the paper, she attempted to duplicate the lake before her. An hour later, Eliza sat back in her chair. Blowing a puff of air from her lips, she attempted to dislodge the wisp of hair tickling her cheek.

"It is no use, Abby. I am hopeless. Joanne has more talent for painting in the tip of her little finger than I."

Abby leaned in for a look. "Well, I must say…" She observed the lake in the distance, bordered with sycamores, then back to Eliza's painting. She pressed her paint-brush against her bottom lip while shaking her head. Eliza swung her hand cloth at her. Abby deflected the swing, giggling, "Truly, Eliza, I have no words."

"Thank you for your confidence, but I warned you." Eliza smiled as she tore the paper from the pad. She crumpled it into a ball before tossing it. Abby ducked just in time for the ball to sail over her head, bouncing across the ground behind her.

"Eliza, don't you want the gentlemen to judge your painting with the others?" Abby smirked. They gazed at each other and dissolved into a fit of giggles. Eliza wiped her eyes. "My talents lie elsewhere, I'm afraid."

Barking dogs could be heard near the stables. "It sounds like the gentlemen have returned," Abby said.

Susan and the dowager countess strolled past, admiring the paintings in turn.

"Eliza, what happened? Aren't you going to participate?" Susan asked, looking at her empty easel.

Eliza glanced at Abby, and they both began to laugh. "I'm afraid my painting didn't turn out," Eliza replied. Standing, she bent over and retrieved her wadded landscape.

"Eliza has decided to give up." Abby tore her painting from her pad and handed it to Susan.

"Painting is not my best talent," Eliza replied, shrugging her shoulders.

The dowager countess clucked her tongue, shaking her head at Eliza's crumpled paper before moving on.

Susan announced that they would be judging the paintings before lunch. With excited giggles, the ladies gathered their picnic baskets along with a blanket and spread them on the lawn.

Eliza and Abby spread a large blanket under a group of trees, their baskets by their side. She watched as gentlemen took slips of paper from a hat held by James. William glanced at his. A frown pulled at the corners of his mouth, and his hair ruffled in the breeze. He gave a quick glance in her direction before heading away from her.

She settled back, disappointed. It was improbable that William would retrieve her number out of the hat, but still, her heart had hoped. A shadow crossed her sight as she shifted her eyes upward. Sir Martin held his number up. His dark eyes had followed her direction toward William.

"May I share your basket, Miss Grant?" He turned his look back to her.

Eliza brightened her smile. "I would love to have you share my basket, Sir Martin, do join us." She pulled plates out of the basket, sorting out food. Sir Martin sat and spread his legs across the blanket. Eliza watched him relax.

Across the yard, her sister Joanne was enjoying her friends. Miss Hardgrave and Miss Shaw giggled at William's antics as he tossed grapes into the air, catching them with his teeth. The captain seemed to be enjoying Miss Sophia's discomfort at having him share lunch with them. Miss Hardgrave batted her eyelashes as she handed the captain a plate of food.

"Miss Grant, you mentioned that you had an aunt and uncle in Bristol?" Sir Martin questioned.

Eliza turned her attention back to her group. "Yes, Sir Martin. My uncle, Mr. Notley, owns a shipping company."

"Donovan Notley is your uncle?" Sir Martin asked, surprise in his voice.

"Yes," replied Eliza. "Do you know him?"

"I should say," Sir Martin replied. "We have been doing business for years. He's the reason I came with Captain Rutley."

"Oh." Eliza, couldn't think of anything else to say.

"Your uncle's looking for some investors for his next shipment to the Americas," Sir Martin continued, his gaze drifting to Captain Rutley across the lawn. "Captain Rutley thought Lord Malmesbury might be interested in investing."

"I'm sure it would be a good investment. My father's always talking about how Uncle Notley seems to be able to turn tobacco into gold."

Sir Martin chuckled at that. "Well, your uncle has done very well for me over the years. His crew seems to like him. He's one of the few honest men in the merchant industry."

"My Aunt Helena has been trying to get me to come to Bristol for several summers now. She wants to bring me out in Bath," Eliza volunteered.

Sir Martin studied her. "But you haven't taken her up on her offer."

Eliza dropped her eyes. "Well, I have not wanted to leave my friends. But now that Abby has had her first

Season in London and Susan is married to Lord Malmesbury...maybe it is time." She gazed out over the lawn. She didn't know why she told all this to Sir Martin. Maybe it was his natural manner and friendship with her aunt and uncle.

Eliza watched William share Miss Shaw's lunch. He continued to show off to the group. She turned. Sir Martin was watching her with his intense brown eyes. He couldn't be more than a few years older than William, yet he seemed more mature.

"Eliza, come play croquet with us. Sir Martin, you are welcome to join us too," Abby said.

Sir Martin smiled before rising. "I'm afraid I've got an appointment at the library, but I thank you for your offer." He bowed and said with a flourish, "Thank you, Miss Grant, for a delicious lunch and pleasant company."

"You're welcome, Sir Martin." Eliza watched as he strolled across the lawn. She mentally compared him to William. She shook off the thought while packing up her lunch basket, then joined Abby at her game.

Conflicting feelings assailed William while he ate lunch with Miss Hardgrave and Eliza's sister. Sir Martin had asked to share Eliza's lunch. What were the odds that he would draw her number? He just couldn't figure out why he was feeling so perturbed and frustrated. This was a new feeling for him. His mind contemplated the matter while he moved through the door. His friends were talking to Sir Martin when he entered the library.

"William, come sit. I think you will be interested in what Sir Martin has to offer," Charles beckoned.

"Gentlemen," Sir Martin began. "I came here because the captain thought you would be interested in some investments that he and I are involved in. As you know, I'm from Bristol, and for years he and I have been investing in shipments of goods from the American colonies."

"A trusted friend of ours has been very profitable over the years. You may not be aware, but since the slave act of 1807, Bristol's economy has been waning. But Mr. Notley's ships have been very profitable in the trade of tobacco and cocoa beans."

"We will be investing in tobacco?" William asked.

"Yes, and other cargo. Mr. Notley has ships making a voyage before winter sets in to pick up tobacco. He's opened up investments for those that would like to help fund the trip," Sir Martin explained.

"James, as you know, I've been able to increase my fortune by my investments with Mr. Notley. I find him very honest, and Virginia's tobacco is of very high-quality," Charles explained.

"What percentage of return would we acquire?" William asked.

"You would receive a percentage based on your investment and the price the tobacco could be sold for once we return to Bristol. The tobacco grown in Virginia fetches an excellent price from the processing companies in Bristol," Sir Martin explained.

"This sounds promising. I would like to meet Mr. Notley and see his fleet," James replied.

"I think that would be a perfect idea. I would like to go to London and talk to my father, then I could meet you in Bristol." William calculated how long he would be in London.

"I found out today that your Miss Grant is Mr. Notley's niece." Sir Martin replied.

"Well," James replied, rubbing his hands together, "that is good news, which might speak well to Mr. Notley's character."

"Yes, Miss Grant told me that Mr. Notley's wife is her father's sister," Sir Martin said.

"Sir Martin and I have known Mr. Notley for years. He has done well with our investments over the years," Charles assured them.

"I agree," Sir Martin said. "William, Lord Malmesbury, you both should come to Bristol. It would be good for you to see Mr. Notley's shipping operation."

The gentlemen continued discussing details of the investment. William knew that his father, Sir George, would be interested. He could leave for London after church services tomorrow and be back within a few weeks.

CHAPTER SIX

*E*liza had taken great care in dressing for the country dance that evening. Guests were arriving, and Eliza could see her father across the room, conversing with the dowager countess. The hall was filling with guests arriving for the evening. A small orchestra sat in the corner. Eliza nodded as Sir Martin approached. "Sir Martin, I would like you to meet my father," she nodded toward the vicar.

"Eliza, dear," her father smiled down at her as she neared the older group.

"Father, may I introduce Sir Martin Wycliffe? Sir Martin, my father, the vicar of our parish, Mr. Owen Grant."

Sir Martin nodded with a slight bow. "Sir, it is a pleasure to meet Miss Grant's father."

"Father, Sir Martin is from Bristol. He knows Aunt Helena and Uncle Donovan."

"You know my sister, Sir Martin?" The vicar's eyes brightened.

"Yes, sir," Sir Martin replied. "I have known them these past years, as Mr. Notley and I have done business together."

William approached Eliza and whispered in her ear. "They're about to announce the winners of the landscape contest."

"Excuse me, Father, Sir Martin." Eliza left her father and Sir Martin discussing Bristol and their connection.

Willian led her to join Abby as they waited for the judge's verdict. She was relieved she had not submitted her awful attempt at painting.

"Ladies and gentlemen," James quieted the group, "we are ready to announce the winner of the landscape painting, of which the young ladies were gracious enough to participate in. The winner will lead the first quadrille tonight."

A young officer stepped forward. Clearing his throat, he said. "I am honored to announce the winner of the landscape painting contest is…. Miss Joanne Grant." The room erupted in applause as Joanne came forward, blushing. The young officer held out his hand to her, and they both advanced to the dance floor and stood at the head of the square.

William turned and bowed. "Eliza, would you honor me with a dance?"

"I would be honored, William." Eliza smiled. They both joined the quadrille next to her sister. Other couples joined in, and the small orchestra began to play. Eliza found herself enjoying the dancing and continued through several rounds as gentlemen asked, until she was tired, finally seeking out Susan for a much-needed rest.

"You're enjoying yourself, I see," Susan said.

"Yes, but it's very warm in here, isn't it?" Eliza waved her hand across her face.

Susan smiled. "Let's take a walk so you can cool down."

They escaped to the terrace. The cool night breeze swept across Eliza's face. She sighed. "This feels good."

"You are not dancing tonight. Are you still feeling sick?" Eliza asked, concerned.

"I am fine. I have a little secret. Only James and I know, and his mother, of course." Susan squeezed her arm. "I am going to have a baby."

While Eliza was thrilled, a little tug pulled at her heart. "Susan, that's wonderful. Are you sure?"

"Yes, I haven't seen the physician yet, but James' mother assures me it is so." Susan's cheeks flushed with happiness.

"When?"

"The dowager tells me she suspects it will be in the spring. So, I will be staying home for a while preparing for my confinement."

"That is wonderful, Susan," Eliza took a breath as they walked inside again.

"How about you, Eliza?" Susan asked. "I noticed you have tender feelings for William."

Eliza stopped, searching her friend's eyes, then relaxed. "Is it that obvious?"

Susan laughed. "No, Eliza, it is not that obvious. I just know you. I'm sure nobody else suspects. Do you know how Williams feels?"

Eliza let out a breath, shaking her head. "William sees us as friends." Eliza turned her eyes to Susan. "Still." Susan patted her arm.

"Did you know Sir Martin is from Bristol? He knows my aunt and uncle." Eliza changed the subject.

"Yes, I know." Susan's smile brought a twinkle to her eyes.

Eliza's lips twisted. She felt uncomfortable discussing her feelings about William. Although she was grateful for Susan's concern. "How is your new project in Fyne Court coming along?" Eliza changed the subject. Susan brightened as she began to tell all the progress that had been accomplished this summer. Fyne Court was Susan's childhood home. Her father had given it to her as a bridal gift upon her marriage to James.

Eliza listened. Susan glowed with excitement as she explained her project. Susan wanted it to be a safe haven for ladies of quality that were being forced to do things their families wanted. Susan's own father had threatened to abandon her if she didn't marry the gentleman he chose.

Eliza was thankful for her own family. She and her sister had a loving father who only wanted the best for them. She knew other girls were not so fortunate.

Sunday morning, the guests attended the local parish where Eliza's father gave a stirring and emotional sermon. William watched as Sir Martin sat with Eliza and her sister. Annoyance rippled through him as he gritted his teeth. He would be glad when Sir Martin returned to Bristol. The party would be breaking up this afternoon, and guests would return home. He attributed his uneasy feeling with his need to go to London.

Parishioners stood and filed into the aisles; Sir Martin followed Eliza and her sister. The vicar greeted them as they exited the chapel.

"Sir Martin, did you enjoy the sermon?" William asked as the two of them walked away from the church.

Sir Martin turned to him, stopping. "I did, Mr. Grant is well versed in the scriptures."

"When will you be returning to Bristol?" William asked, tensing as he waited for a reply.

"I will be leaving in the morning. I have other business I must attend to."

William felt relief. "I wish you a good trip, then, Sir Martin."

"Miss Grant tells me she may make a trip to Bristol to visit her aunt. I hope to see her there."

William felt alarmed, again. "Eliza," William stopped. "I mean Miss Grant, to visit Bristol?"

Sir Martin raised a brow as he studied him. "Is there something between you and Miss Grant? I would hate to presume."

William's alarm grew. He must not compromise Eliza any further after Sir Martin witnessed their playfulness in the garden and seeing his relationship with Eliza's family. He did not want any ill will to follow her. "I assure you, sir, Miss Grant and I are just friends, as I have told you. We have been these many years, along with my sister, Lady Abigale."

Sir Martin seemed to accept his answer, nodding as they continued to walk.

"I am leaving for London this afternoon; I want to talk with my father about your investment plan," William stated, changing the subject. Then he excused himself from Sir Martin, and he looked around for his sister.

"Abby, I'm leaving for London to visit Father. The carriage will take you and Aunt Lucy back to Bowood House."

"You're leaving for London now?"

"I have some business to discuss with Father, and I'm anxious to leave. If I leave now, I can be in London tomorrow evening."

Eliza gazed around the churchyard her eyes adjusting to the sunlight. Parishioners were gathered in groups, talking. William was talking with Sir Martin across the yard so she walked toward them. She heard her name as she neared. Pausing as William exclaimed, "I assure you, sir, Eliza and I are *just friends* as I have told you and have been for many years."

Eliza's cheeks flushed, and she quickly turned away, retracing her steps. She had not meant to eavesdrop on their conversation. She looked to find her sister while anxiously pondering the meaning behind his words, *just friends*. Had she misread his actions? Hadn't he been about to kiss her in the garden? William had been so attentive throughout the party, helping her from her horse, dancing with her. A flush came to her cheeks. He had been polite to other guests as well. Maybe she had only wished it.

She noticed Joanne in the yard with her friends, Sophia keeping them animated. She hesitated to interrupt and meandered over towards Susan and James instead. She scanned the crowd frantically. He said he was leaving for London. She needed to talk to him before he left. Turning, she walked back through the crowd of people.

"Abby, have you seen William?" Eliza asked.

"He left for London."

"He left for London now? Today?"

"Yes, he needed to discuss some business with our father," Abby said.

That's strange, Eliza thought. "It couldn't wait until after the house party broke up?"

"You know William," Abby said. "We never know what he's going to do."

Eliza was disappointed even though she knew she shouldn't feel this way. William needn't say goodbye every time he left town. They were only friends, after all. At least that's what he said. Frustration bubbled up from inside. Why was she doing this to herself? Waiting around, hoping William's feelings would change. It was apparent she had been a fool, wasting the last few years pining for him. Maybe it was time to visit her aunt.

"Abby, my Aunt Helena, has been begging me to come to Bristol to live with her and my uncle. She wants to take me to Bath for the Season."

"Eliza, that's wonderful." Abby reached for her hands, giving them a squeeze. "Are you going to go?"

"I have been thinking about it," Eliza bit her lip. "Although I hesitate to leave my friends and Joanne. But now that Susan is married, and you're going off to London for the Season..."

"Of course, you should go, Eliza," Abby squeezed her fingers tighter. "I wish I could go to Bath for a Season."

"Why would you want to go to Bath when your father is paying for a Season in London?" Eliza gently removed her hands from Abby's before she cut off her circulation.

"I've already been to London, and my father expects

me to find a husband this Season. If you are going to be in Bath, that's where I want to be. Maybe I could find more interesting gentlemen there," Abby flushed with excitement.

"I wouldn't know anything about that. I have never had a Season, so I'm not sure what kind of gentlemen you will meet."

"Eliza, you will love it. New clothes, parties, dancing, visiting, making new friends..." Abby sighed. "If you are lucky, you will find love. Just like Susan and James."

"Susan and James did not meet in London," Eliza crooked her brow. "And what does luck have to do with it?"

"That is true. But you need to be seen to find love. Get out, meet people, go to parties. There are not many parties around here."

Eliza laughed at Abby's logic, shaking her head. "Abby, you've convinced me. My father will certainly be happy. He's been trying to get me to visit my aunt for several years now."

Eliza would write her tonight. Before she changed her mind.

CHAPTER SEVEN

*E*liza wrote to her Aunt Helena before she lost her nerve, posting the letter immediately before she changed her mind. There, it was done. There was no turning back. She just needed to wait for her aunt's reply.

It had been a week since William left for London, and already, she missed him. She would go crazy if she did not do something to keep her mind occupied. She marched off to the kitchen where Mrs. Baker had left several loaves of bread and a fresh-baked molasses cake. Eliza pulled a basket from the pantry and carefully wrapped a loaf of bread with cheese and fruit. She had just finished slicing several pieces of cake when Joanne entered the kitchen. Eliza wrapped the cake in parchment, and tucked everything neatly inside, placing a napkin over the top of the basket.

"I'm going to visit the widow Reese. Would you like

to come with me?" Eliza picked up the molasses cake and returned it to the pantry.

"Yes, I'll grab my cloak." Joanne hurried from the kitchen.

Visiting the widow Reese took several hours of Eliza's day and significantly reduced her worry. She and Joanne continued to visit parishioners each day, which gave Eliza a feeling of satisfaction and calm. At the end of the week, she and Joanne returned home with another empty basket. A large carriage stood outside the vicarage.

"Aunt Helena is here." Her sister picked up her pace and ran to the door.

What could this mean? Eliza expected a letter from her aunt, not a visit.

Aunt Helena was drinking tea with her father. When Eliza entered the parlor, Joanne was wrapping her aunt in a warm embrace.

"Look at you, Joanne," her aunt held Joanne back to examine her. "You have turned into such a beautiful young lady."

"Aunt Helena, you came! I thought you would write a letter."

Her aunt raised her eyes. "Eliza, I see you've turned into a lovely lady as well." Aunt Helena turned to her father. "Owen, they are both so beautiful. Eliza, you look so much like your mother." Her aunt's eyes teared.

"Yes, she does." Her father beamed. "Girls, come join us for tea."

"I didn't expect you so soon, Aunt Helena." Eliza sat, accepting the cup her sister had poured for her.

"I was so excited to receive your letter stating that you were going to come to Bristol." Her aunt patted her hand. "I didn't want to take a chance on you changing your mind. Besides, you need a chaperone, so I thought I would bring you myself and visit with my brother." Aunt Helena smiled at her father.

"You are always welcome here, Helena."

Aunt Helena was still handsome, her dark hair untouched by gray, with stunning blue eyes. Her smile was infectious. Eliza knew not to let her aunt's looks deceive her. Underneath that sweet exterior was a heart of steel. When she got something into her head, she was very determined to see it through to completion. And her aunt was determined to procure a good marriage for Eliza, and when that was accomplished, Joanne would be her next project.

The formalities over, her aunt suggested they make a trip to the modistes. "I want to buy you both a few new gowns." She insisted, giving her brother a look, that said she would not be deterred. Her father capitulated without a fight.

Within three days, Aunt Helena had her trunks sent ahead to Bristol. Abby and Susan both came for tea. "Eliza, I am so excited for you." Abby nearly bounced in her chair. "To have your aunt prepared to give you a Season in Bath." Her eyes shined.

"Now you must promise to write. Eliza," Susan prompted.

"I will. I will be home for Christmas and the New Year. My aunt has plans to keep me entertained this winter, and I'm sure it includes more shopping." Her eyes brightened, as she stood and turned a full circle for her friends to see.

"I thought that was new," Abby exclaimed.

"My aunt insisted we go to town yesterday, and she managed to wrangle three new gowns for Joanne and me as well as new gloves and a hat."

"You look lovely," Susan said. "Although we will miss you, I am glad your aunt is so attentive to your needs."

"Oh, Eliza, we will miss you so. But remember, you promised to write. I must hear about all your new beaus."

"Yes, I will, Abby. Although I doubt there will be any beaus, as you say." Eliza would miss her friends. She promised herself she would have no regrets. Besides, it was only for the season, she would be home in the spring.

Her friends stayed an extra half hour before bidding Eliza farewell with more promises to keep in touch.

Her aunt's carriage pulled away from the vicarage the next morning. Eliza watched her sister and father from the carriage window. Her heart melted as the vicarage receded from her view. She missed them already. Was she making a mistake, leaving her heart behind? What would William think when he returned to find her gone? Would he miss her?

Aunt Helena's home was situated in a fashionable part of town. The bustle of the city with its modern facilities surprised her. "I had no idea Bristol had grown so much, Aunt Helena,"

"Yes, my dear, it has. Mind you, things have been hard since the abolishment of the slave trade," Aunt Helena explained, "but Mr. Notley never ascribed to the sale of humans, bless him. Tobacco, sugar, and cocoa from the West Indies and America have seen a good living for us."

Eliza was amazed that her aunt knew about her husband's shipping business.

"Aunt Helena, you know about Uncle Notley's business dealings?"

Her aunt gave her a sharp look. "Yes, dear, I do. Does that surprise you?"

"I believe you have the head for business, Aunt Helena. What surprises me is that Uncle Notley would talk to you about it."

"Do not be surprised, when your uncle and I were young and first married, I helped him with the books." Her aunt smiled and gazed out the window as if remembering. "Sir George Phelips gave us a loan to buy that first ship after we were married."

"Sir George?" Eliza's interest was peaked. "William's father?"

"Yes, dear, just like he gave your father the living of the parish along with a home at the vicarage when he married your mother. It's a good living."

Yes, it was a good living, Eliza thought, but she'd had no idea Sir George had that close of a connection with her family.

"My father, your grandfather, and Sir George were friends. My father saved Sir George's life, and after that, they became friends for the rest of their lives."

Her grandfather had died before Eliza was born. She had never heard this story. Maybe that's why Sir George always allowed Abby and William to be her playmates.

"I am surprised your father never told you this story," Aunt Helena replied.

"Father is so busy with his sermons and visits to his parishioners, he doesn't talk much about his past," Eliza explained, "and I'm afraid I have not asked about it."

"Well, dear, young ladies have other things on their minds to be sure."

The carriage stopped in front of a large house. Eliza was impressed. A finely liveried groom opened the door while an attendant helped her aunt as she stepped out. A very tall black man opened the door as they entered the entryway. Eliza peered down a long hallway which extended all the way to the back of the house, which she found very unusual.

"Ramsey," her aunt said motioning to the man, "this

is my niece, Miss Eliza Grant. Please have Mrs. Ramsey inform Ruby that her mistress is here and to come to the parlor to meet Miss Eliza."

"Yes, my lady," the butler replied as he took her aunt's hat and gloves.

"Ramsey!" her aunt exclaimed in exasperation. "How many times must I inform you? I am not a lady."

"Yes, ma'am," the butler replied.

"Please have the cook send up a tray. Thank you, Ramsey."

The black butler bowed and moved to leave the room. Her aunt shook her head as she settled into a soft couch that molded around her. Eliza sat next to her, adjusting the lace pillows that decorated the furniture. Eliza tried to keep her face neutral.

"I see you are surprised, Eliza," her aunt said.

"Your butler Ramsey... is he a slave?" Eliza whispered.

A trill of laughter escaped from her aunt. "Oh, no, my dear. Mr. and Mrs. Ramsey are free. They have been with me these past ten years."

"Mrs. Ramsey?" Eliza's voice squeaked. "Your butler is married?" She had never seen a married butler before.

"Yes, Mrs. Ramsey is my housekeeper, and her husband is the butler. It is unusual, I know, but it has worked out very well for us. You will find a lot of things in this household that may seem foreign."

A servant knocked, entering with a tray which was placed on a wheeled cart by the door.

"You may place the cart here by my side," her aunt instructed the servant. The smell of tea wafted through the air as Eliza realized how hungry she was. Her aunt poured her a cup, adding sugar and cream. Eliza could smell spices as the steam tickled her nose, and she sipped the hot liquid. Her eyes widened in surprise. "It's a special spice blend we get from India."

"I like it." Eliza took another drink.

"I have assigned Ruby to be your lady's maid. She will need some training, but she learns quickly. Ruby's a very bright girl and eager to please. If you like her, you may take her with you to your marriage."

A knock sounded, and a very tall, elegant woman entered the room. A young girl with the most beautiful golden complexion followed.

"Miss Ruby is here, madame."

"Thank you, Mrs. Ramsey," her aunt replied.

Mrs. Ramsey retreated, leaving the shy maid waiting, observing Eliza under her lashes. She wore a gray and white uniform, her dark hair pulled back in a severe bun at the nape of her neck, a white cap covering the crown of her head.

"Come here, Ruby, so Miss Eliza can get a better look at you," her aunt waved her hand. The pretty girl moved across the carpet to stand before Eliza.

"That's better. Now, Ruby, Miss Eliza is going to help train you to be a lady's maid, so you be sure to follow her directions. Then, maybe she will keep you on after she leaves us."

Ruby stifled a giggle as she looked at Eliza. She gave her a slight curtsy, her wide eyes never leaving Eliza.

Aunt Helena shook her head, trying not to smile. "That will be all Ruby. You may go to Miss Eliza's room and take care of her trunks."

"Yes, ma'am." Ruby quickly moved back across the carpet, slipping through the door.

"Thank you, Aunt Helena, I think Ruby will do just fine."

"The girl can be flighty when she gets excited. She has a good head on her shoulders and when she gets to know you, she should settle down."

Eliza relaxed and finished her drink, eating several sandwich wedges that satisfied her hunger.

"Now, Eliza dear. You go and get some rest. Mrs. Ramsey will show you to your room. Dinner is at six, and you'll be able to meet Mr. Notley. He's very excited to see how you've grown."

Eliza remembered her uncle as an amiable man who adored her aunt. Her steps began to drag as she followed the housekeeper to her room. A rest would be nice. She yawned.

CHAPTER EIGHT

*R*uby helped Eliza undress. She slipped into a dressing gown and dropped onto the big four-poster bed. Her eyes closed, not realizing how tired she was until her head hit the pillow. It was an unusual household, Eliza thought as she drifted off to sleep.

Eliza awoke to her maid, rattling around in her room. She shifted her weight and sat up in bed blinking. A moment passed before her head cleared, and she remembered she was in Bristol with her aunt.

"Miss," her maid came to her bedside. "Madam has asked me to help you get ready for dinner. It's five o'clock, and dinner will be served in an hour."

"Thank you, Ruby." Eliza yawned, swinging her legs from the bed. Her nap had only made her head foggier.

With Ruby's help, Eliza entered the parlor at ten minutes to six. A group of people milled about talking.

She hadn't expected guests for dinner, brushing her hands along her skirt, thankful for her new gowns. Her Aunt Helena waved her over as she crossed the threshold.

"Eliza, dear," her aunt swept by her side, bringing her into the room.

"Is this our Eliza?" Uncle Notley exclaimed, taking her hands. He gazed her up and down. "You are right, my dear. She has grown into a lovely lady."

Eliza felt heat rising to her cheeks as her uncle gushed over her in the unknown company.

"Now Mr. Notley, you're embarrassing our girl," her aunt said as she guided Eliza across the room. "I want you to meet some of our friends."

Her aunt introduced her to an older couple. "Mr. and Mrs. Dalton, I'd like you to meet my niece, Miss Eliza grant."

"It is nice to meet you," Eliza gave a slight curtsy.

The older couple nodded. Eliza thought they were a little stiff; penetrating eyes examined her. She turned her attention to a pretty girl about her age. A young man stood by their side, his mouth a straight line.

"And this, my dear, is Miss Isabella Dalton and her brother, Mr. Dalton."

"It is nice to meet you, Miss Eliza," Isabella's eyes sparkled as she welcomed Eliza. Her brother nodded and turned his attention elsewhere.

"Now Eliza, I hope that you and Miss Isabella will become friends," her aunt patted her arm.

"Oh, I'm sure we will, Mrs. Notley," Miss Dalton assured her aunt. Her friendly smile widened across her face.

Eliza blinked as she looked at this beautiful woman standing before her. She didn't appear to be much older than herself. Her hair was done up with shiny curls falling out of a braid high upon her head. Eyes glowed through thick eyelashes, making them appear larger.

Eliza returned her smile. "Yes, I hope we will."

Her brother had left them to talk to another gentleman across the room.

"You and Sir Martin know each other, don't you, Eliza?" her aunt asked.

She smiled up into Sir Martin's face. "We do," Sir Martin replied. "How are you, Miss Grant? I trust your trip was good."

"Yes, sir, very good. Aunt Notley's carriage was well sprung, and your roads are very well maintained here in Bristol."

The group laughed. "Yes, you are right, Miss Grant. We have had many compliments on the roads here in Bristol." Sir Martin smiled down at her. "It is the asphaltum," he whispered.

The company was interrupted by the announcement from the butler that dinner was served.

Eliza found dinner an informal affair. She sat between Sir Martin and Miss Isabella, her aunt and uncle sat at opposite heads of the table. A soup was served first, followed by a well-flavored lamb and a variety of vegetables. The company conversed between courses as they ate. No subject seemed to be taboo, even with the ladies' present.

"Asphaltum, Sir Martin? What is that?" Eliza was curious. It was a word she hadn't heard before.

"Bitumen is mixed with gravel aggregate, Miss Grant, to form the road base you so admired. It is referred to as asphaltum."

"How clever. I knew bitumen was used in my uncle's ships for waterproofing, yet I had no idea of its use on roads. It surely would be nice in the country where the roads are most horrible in the winter months."

"I must confess, I am surprised at your interest in roads, Miss Grant."

"You are surprised that a woman would be interested in other things besides fripperies, Sir Martin?" Eliza's smile softening the question.

"No, Miss Grant. I am happy to see you possess a mind as curious as your aunt's," he confessed.

"Miss Grant, it must be so exciting to live in the country," Miss Isabella spoke from her other side. "What is it like?" Her eyes shone.

Eliza laughed, "Well, I don't know how it compares to living in the city. I've only lived in the country. But I do love it. It's greener, and in our small parish, everyone knows everybody. It is quite cozy." Eliza thought of her sister and her friends. She missed them already. "It can be quite frustrating during the rainy season. The roads get muddy and bogged down, making it hard to travel in the winter, not like your roads here in Bristol."

"Oh, it sounds exciting. I would love to visit the country. I've only lived in the city."

Eliza liked her. Miss Isabella had an exuberant innocence. "Call me, Eliza. I believe we shall be friends."

"Oh, yes, and you shall call me Isabella."

When dinner ended, her uncle and aunt led the group into the parlor. Eliza was surprised that the men joined the ladies for their after-dinner brandy, the women did not seem to mind.

"Isabella, play for us on the pianoforte," Mrs. Dalton demanded from across the room. Isabella jumped, "Yes, ma'am."

Isabella rose and walked over to the pianoforte. She sat, leafing through the sheet music before picking a song, her shiny eyes concentrating on the page before her.

Eliza watched the others in the room. Her aunt and uncle were playing cards with Mr. and Mrs. Dalton. Sir Martin and the young Mr. Dalton were drinking brandy by the fireplace, conversing quietly. She was surprised no one seemed to notice Isabella's distress at her mother's sharp command, not even her brother. So Eliza rose and slid onto the bench seat next to Isabella. Reaching up, she turned the pages of the music. Isabella glanced at Eliza, giving her a slight grin, her eyes pooling with moisture.

William had spent three weeks in London conferring with his father. The investment in Mr. Notley's fleet looked to be sound. His father couldn't leave London but had every confidence in his friend Mr. Notley, but William still wanted to visit Bristol and see the operation for himself. After all, Sir Martin was expecting his visit.

William arrived back to Montacute within a couple of days. He would meet with his steward to see that everything was settled for the winter, before planning his trip to Bristol.

Eliza kept coming to mind. He still felt unsettled about Sir Martin's question about his relationship with her, outside church that Sunday. That day he'd left for London, had thrown him into a turmoil of conflicting feelings. He hoped a visit to the vicarage would help. He hated to admit he missed Eliza, and he felt guilty at not saying goodbye before leaving for London. Why he should, he didn't understand. It had never bothered him before.

The meeting with his steward lasted a couple of hours, and now, with his business handled, he went to change before his visit to Eliza's. His valet finished tying his cravat as he pulled his waistcoat down, then he instructed him to notify the groom.

"As you wish, my lord."

Aunt Lucy was still in the breakfast parlor when he

entered. "William, I'm glad to see you're back from London. How is your father?"

"He's well, Aunt Lucy. Working as usual. I'm going to be going to Bristol at the end of the week to check out the investment we discussed." William filled a plate with eggs, two slices of bacon, and dry toast from the buffet.

"I thought I would go over to the vicarage. Didn't Eliza say that her aunt and uncle were the Notleys that owned the shipping firm?" A footman poured coffee in a cup, placing it beside him.

"I believe so, my dear. I heard Eliza talking to Sir Martin about the acquaintance they shared."

"Then maybe Eliza's father will have some information about Mr. Notley's firm," William mused. He finished his breakfast in a few quick bites, drinking the hot liquid carefully before leaving his aunt.

William left his horse at the stables with the boy. A maid answered the door at the vicarage.

"Is Mr. Grant in?"

"This way, sir." The maid bobbed a curtsy and led him into the parlor. Sun poured in through the south window, illuminating dust particles floating through the beams of light.

"I will let the vicar know you are here, sir."

William sat in a comfortable chair; the sun warming

the room.

"William, my boy, it's good to see you." The vicar beamed as he approached.

William stood, giving the vicar a firm shake of the hand.

"I hear you have been in London. How is Sir George?"

"He's very well, sir. I've just spent the last few weeks with him. He is working as hard as ever. I could not convince him to come home."

"Oh, yes. My daughters chide me for working too hard as well. But it keeps our minds busy." The vicar tapped his temple and waved William to sit.

William noted the changes in Eliza's father as he returned to his seat. Of medium height, his graying hair was once the same colour as Eliza's. He was growing older, as was his own father. But still the vicar's kind, penetrating eyes missed nothing.

"What brings you to the parish today William?"

"I understand Mr. Notley is your brother-in-law," William replied.

"Ah, yes, Mr. Notley. Yes, he is a fine man. He married my sister Helena. They live in Bristol you know."

"I see. I ask because Sir Martin has proposed an investment in Mr. Notley's next ship, leaving for the Americas. My father has confidence in him. But I felt I should see his operation and determine the risk of this venture myself."

"I agree with Sir George. Mr. Notley is a man of good character. But it would be wise to meet him with him first. See his business for yourself. It's always good to do your due diligence."

William nodded in agreement. "Is Eliza in?" William tried to keep his voice nonchalant.

The vicar's brow wrinkled. "No, Eliza is in Bristol. She's gone to live with my sister for a time."

A tightness in his chest returned. "Eliza's in Bristol?"

The vicar chuckled. "My sister's been trying to get her to come for a few years now. I suppose she finally thought it was time. With Miss Hamilton married to Lord Malmesbury, and your sister Abby going off to London for the Season, there is not much around here anymore. I expect she will come home for a visit at Christmas."

William did not know what to say. He felt stunned. Eliza was in Bristol, living with her aunt?

"Thank you for your help," William was finally able to reply.

"You're welcome. Come by anytime." The vicar walked him out.

William contemplated what the vicar had told him as he neared his home. The leaves had started to fall. It was October, and soon it would be snowing. The vicar said Eliza might be home for Christmas and the New Year. His heart sank as an odd twinge of disappointment settled in. He pushed his mount faster toward home.

CHAPTER NINE

*W*illiam searched out his sister as soon as he reached the house. He found her in the back parlor, his Aunt Lucy working embroidery while Abby sat at her desk amongst piles of papers. He tumbled into his favorite leather chair. Swinging his ankle over his knee, he fiddled with the leather strap on his boot.

"Abby, when did Eliza go to Bristol?" he asked.

Abby looked up, her eyes meeting his. "Eliza?"

William tried to keep his patience in check. "Yes, when did Eliza go to Bristol?" His boot tapped the floor as he tried to remain nonchalant.

"Oh, well, I think it's been about three or four weeks, hasn't it, Aunt Lucy?"

His aunt looked up from her embroidery. "Yes dear, it was just after Lady Susan's house party."

"The vicar said she was going to live there with her aunt and uncle." William looked concerned.

Abby brightened. "Yes, isn't that exciting?" Abby went on without taking a breath. "Apparently, her aunt and uncle have wanted Eliza to come to Bristol for several years."

"But why?" William's heart rate picked up, doing double time.

"Eliza's aunt is taking her under her wing. She's going to sponsor her for a Season in Bath to find her a husband."

A husband? Why couldn't she find one here? Susan had.

Abby shuffled through a stack of letters. "I know it's here… oh, yes, here it is." Abby pulled up a letter from the pile of papers. "Here," Abby scanned the letter. "Eliza writes…" she paused, "'I have met the most wonderful friend. Her name is Isabella. We do everything together. She reminds me of you, Abby, and she is so much fun. I am so glad I met her, for it would be so lonely here without you.'" Abby looked from the letter and smiled. "I should like to meet this Isabella."

William relaxed a little in his seat only to tense up in the next paragraph as Abby continued.

"'I have met the most wonderful gentlemen. A Mr. Templeton comes by to take me driving out to the park, and a Mr. Dowding comes by and drives me to the docks, to show me Uncle Notley's ships, which are quite interesting as the cargo is loaded off and on the ships.

It's quite funny to see them fighting over who's going to take me driving. But Sir Martin is a jewel and has helped me adjust to the company of gentlemen. They have given me such confidence.'"

"Isn't it romantic?" Abby sighed, holding the letter to her.

William huffed, "I think you have stars in your eyes, little sister." He sunk further into his chair. "You think everything is romantic."

Abby scowled at her brother. "Oh? Well, listen to this, "'With Isabella's help and the gentlemen callers, I have improved my dancing and social skills. Aunt Helena mentioned the other day that if my popularity continues, I may be snatched up before I have a chance to go to Bath. I find this quite impossible.'" Abby gave her brother a quick look before continuing. "'But I find myself growing quite comfortable in their company and can now hold up my end of the conversation. I feel much more prepared to start a courtship should the right gentleman come calling, of course.'"

"Courting? Eliza is courting?" William felt his breath seeping from his lungs, at the same time his heart raced like a steam engine.

"Well, she hasn't said, but I am sure it will be soon with all those gentlemen calling," Abby replied.

"I pay attention to her, I dance with her, we talk," William complained.

"Not that kind of attention, William. You tease and treat her as a sister. Women want to be courted and appreciated by gentlemen who make their heart flutter. It is time Eliza found a husband." Abby gave her brother a smirk as she waved the letter at him. "It will not be long before Eliza is married, just like Susan, and this time, I shall be in attendance at her wedding."

Abby tossed the letter back on her pile. "Oh, Aunt Lucy, do you think father will let me have a Season in Bath this year?"

Aunt Lucy shook her head and clucked, "I'm afraid not, Abby, as your father is in London and I don't think you'll be able to extract him."

William slapped his palms on the chair. "This is quite ridiculous. I'm leaving for Bristol tonight."

Abby and Aunt Lucy gaped. "But William, you just arrived. I thought you would be leaving next week?"

"A week may be too late Aunt Lucy. I have Eliza's reputation to protect. I will meet her uncle and discern his character for myself. Letting Eliza prance around the city with a strange gentleman…" William muttered.

"What are you talking about? I'm shocked at that accusation," Abby rallied. "These gentlemen are not strangers, and Eliza would not prance around the city. They are friends of Sir Martin's."

"Exactly, how much do we know of Sir Martin?"

Abby fumed. "He is friends with Charles and James. Is that not enough?"

"Maybe, but I will see for myself," William declared as he turned to leave. "If anyone is going to be courting Eliza, it will be me," he mumbled under his breath.

He heard his aunt admonish his sister before he closed the door.

"Abby, enough. Let Eliza and William work this out."

He would work it out alright, William just hoped he wouldn't arrive too late.

William left Montacute after a quick noon meal, in a curricle accompanied by his man. He told himself it was faster. He had Eliza's security in mind, only a few days, just until he knew Eliza was in safe hands. She did not understand how dangerous a gentleman looking for a moneyed wife could be.

William knew Eliza had a dowry. Her father had put money away for both his daughters. He did not know how much, but if her uncle had added to it, it would be a considerable sum. Gentlemen preyed on women, unscrupulous men with pockets to let. Had he not seen them in London last season?

William and James saved his betrothed, Susan, before she could be compromised by an untrustworthy suitor that would not take no for an answer. William was determined the same fate would not fall to Eliza. He had no intention of permitting her to fall under the spell of a conniving gentlemen.

If he thought about it, he'd always had a crush on Eliza. It was a boyhood thing which he hadn't given much thought at the time. All boys had a crush at one time or another. Eliza was older than his sister, but the three of them had spent more time together than he had with the boys in the neighborhood. William had been tutored until it was time to leave for school.

But why did he feel like he had been sucker punched? He felt a surge of protectiveness —possibly even possessiveness. Her eyes still haunted him when he'd held her by the tree, embarrassed when Sir Martin came upon them. Eliza had never been angry with him before. He didn't like the feeling.

Sir Martin was in Bristol as well. His heart quickened at the thought. William could not get to Bristol soon enough.

CHAPTER TEN

*E*liza had invited Isabella to go to the market on Corn Street with her in her aunt's gig. She was getting quite proficient at handling the horse in the city.

Isabella arrived, escorted by her brother, who left as soon as Isabella was in her aunt's house. The day was warm, with a few clouds. Eliza had put on her green velvet cloak with the fur-lined hood her aunt had bought for her. "Isabella, you look very nice today."

"Thank you, Eliza. I am looking forward to a visit to town without my brother in tow." She giggled.

"Aunt Helena is letting us use the gig."

"Your carriage is here, Miss Grant," the butler announced.

"Thank you, Mr. Ramsey."

"Eliza," Isabella commented as Eliza guided the gig into the road. "I am so glad you came to Bristol. It's been so nice to have a friend."

Eliza turned. "But surely you have friends here. After all, you've lived here all your life."

"Oh, I had plenty of friends while I was in school, but since I've come out, well, my parents can be rather restrictive."

Eliza looked into Isabella's eyes and saw sadness there. "I only have my father. I don't remember my mother. She died when I was young."

"Oh, I'm sorry," Isabella touched her arm, concern on her face.

"It's fine, I don't remember her much, and my father has been the best of parents, and I have had Aunt Helena. She dotes on my sister and me terribly."

"I can't help but wish my parents were more like your aunt and uncle."

Eliza laughed. "Well, I think my aunt and uncle are quite unique. They do love each other; I can see that. Aunt Helena tells me my parents loved each other as well. I can believe that." Eliza said, "because my father is so loving to my sister and myself. He just wants us to be happy and find someone that will love us like he loved my mother."

Isabella shook her head. "How would that be?" She sighed.

Eliza could not understand how two parents could be so oblivious to such a beautiful daughter, and her brother acted like she was invisible most of the time. She was reminded of William and his love for his sister, Abby.

William. She shook her head and put him out of her mind. Pulling the gig against the boardwalk in front of the Corn Exchange, Eliza and Isabella left their conveyance with a young man who took the leads and tied them to a post.

The inside of the exchange was an open courtyard lined with columned archways between which were shops brimming with goods where they spent the day shopping. "Isabella, shall we stop in at the chocolate shop? The chocolate here in Bristol is the best I have tasted."

Isabella agreed.

A waiter poured the creamy brown liquid in their cups while they sat at a small outdoor table. Just as Eliza lifted her warm cup to her lips, a small black boy bumped the table brushing against Eliza's skirt as he quickly scooted underneath. His big eyes beamed up at her before he dropped the tablecloth, disappearing from view.

A loud commotion followed in the boy's wake as a large, burly man charged towards them, yelling what she figured was the boy's name. Eliza held her cup tight as the table jiggled not daring to put it down. Isabella's eyes widened from the other side.

"Where are you, you little scoundrel? When I get a hold of you."

Eliza was astonished at the expletives spewing from his mouth. Before she could stop him, the man reached under the table where two black toes peeked out from under the cloth.

"Got ya, you little squirt." The gruff man hauled the young boy out, shaking him violently. "Thought you could escape, did you? Your hide is mine when we get you back home." The dirty man began to drag the little boy across the courtyard.

Eliza's temper rose at the treatment of the child being abused. She stood before taking an abrupt step toward him. "Sir, how dare you treat the child in such a dreadful manner!"

He swung around and snarled, "Ye have no right, ma'am, to interfere." Spittle spewed from his lips. "He is my property and there ain't nothing you can do about it." He began to advance towards Eliza, pulling the boy with him.

Elisa set her cup on the table and stepped forward, determined to protect the boy, when she was abruptly caught by the elbow and firmly pulled back. "The lady is just concerned about the child," Sir Martin spoke, addressing the brute.

"Well," the man replied, turning, "I want no abolitionists interfering with my property," he mumbled taking in Sir Martin's attire. He backed off, retreating, taking the boy with him.

"Sir Martin, the boy could not be more than five or six. What does he mean to do?"

"The boy is his, Miss Grant, the man is well within his rights. It was dangerous to confront him." Sir Martin glanced around. The onlookers went back to their own affairs as if nothing had happened.

"I see your point. Sir Martin." Eliza backed away. The young boy turned and flashed a smile and a wink in her direction. Then he was gone, disappearing around the corner. It appeared the young boy was not as upset as she. She agreed to let Sir Martin escort them back to their gig as he retrieved their packages. "Thank you for your help, Sir Martin."

Eliza was glad that she'd been raised in the country where the scenes that she experienced today were few. She could only think of London and the squalor of the slums she'd heard about as her heart went out to the young boy.

Sir Martin nodded. "Miss Grant, Miss Dalton. Might I take you both for a ride in the park Sunday?"

"I would like that, Sir Martin," Eliza replied, thankful he had stepped in before she had been accosted. Somehow, she didn't think the brute cared that she was a lady and it may have turned unpleasant.

Sir Martin tipped his hat and walked down the boardwalk as Eliza maneuvered the gig back onto the street and made for her aunt's home.

"Did that vile man own the little boy?" Eliza asked

"I am afraid he did," Isabella replied.

"Why did he call me an abolitionist?"

Isabella giggled, easing the tension Eliza felt. "Because you were trying to help the black boy, only abolitionists interfere with a slave owner."

William situated himself at a local coaching inn after arriving in Bristol, sending word to Sir Martin that he had come, and would Sir Martin call on him at the coffeehouse on Corn Street? William resisted the urge to locate Mr. Notley's address and call on him right then. It would be indiscreet of him to just show up at the door.

He had a chance to think on his way to Bristol. Maybe he had been a little too impulsive leaving so quickly without a plan. But the thought of Eliza being taken advantage of, caused such anxiety, he had needed to do something.

He bought a paper from a boy on the street, tossing him a coin, and proceeded to the coffee house located at the Corn Exchange, one that had been recommended by the hostler at the inn.

"William." Sir Martin approached, removing his hat. "I see you have made it to our fair city at last. I was glad to receive your note." He laid the hat on the table as he sat down. William had liked the fellow. His irritation only surfaced when Sir Martin had shown interest in Eliza. He was not ready to examine those feelings.

"I have, Sir Martin. I have just been to London, where my father sends his greetings. I would like to meet with Mr. Notley and get information about his shipping operation."

"I have anticipated as much, so I sent word to Mr. Notley at his office. He is expecting us. Why don't we take a drive by the shipyards on the way? I'd like you to see Mr. Notley's fleet. Two of the ships are awaiting cargo before they set sail to the Americas."

The dock was bustling when they arrived. The port was situated in an inland bay where the ships were protected from the rough open sea, Sir Martin explained. William was impressed with the two ships belonging to Mr. Notley. They weighed two hundred and fifty tons with three masts, able to make the voyage in six weeks under good sail.

"Would you like to go aboard?"

William nodded, eager to see the inner workings. Sir Martin explained finished goods were taken to the West Indies and America and raw materials brought back on the return voyage, maximizing profits as well as supplying much needed finished goods to the islands. Sir Martin's knowledge of the business impressed William.

Mr. Notley's office was not far from the ports situated in a three-story building. William climbed the stairs to the first floor, entering the large office. Wooden cabinets lined the walls. A stately gentleman extended both his hands, shaking William's vigorously.

"You must be William? It's a pleasure to meet Sir George's son." The gentleman greeted him with much enthusiasm.

"My father sends his regards." William nodded, assuming he was addressing Mr. Notley.

"Mr. Notley," Sir Martin commented, "meet

William Phelips. We have been down to the docks to see your ships; I have taken William on a tour."

"Very good, very good," Mr. Notley nodded. "I trust Sir Martin has answered any questions you may have?"

"I found him well-informed," William assured Mr. Notley.

"Ah, good, good."

Eliza's uncle soon had William bent over a table, maps and papers were strewn about while he explained the merchant business, giving William a general sense of his character. Despite Mr. Notley's general sunny temperament and a liberal supply of good sense, he could see his business had prospered through hard work and honesty, generally lacking in the industry. William had already decided to invest, but his coming here had more to do with Eliza and seeing that she was safe, he admitted to himself.

"Well William, do you have any more questions for me?" Mr. Notley asked.

"I am quite impressed, Mr. Notley. I see now why Captain Rutley has recommended you so highly."

Mr. Notley shook his head, smiling. "That is good, that is good. I would like you to come to dinner tonight. We are having guests, and my wife would be honored to meet you."

"Thank you, I would like that."

CHAPTER ELEVEN

*W*illiam rode with Sir Martin to the Notley's home later that evening. It was located in what Sir Martin referred to as the crescent, a fashionable area situated on a hill outside of town. It appeared to avoid the noise and clamor of the city below.

The house wasn't large by William's standards, but it was situated nicely. Entering the foyer, he discovered it was more significant than it appeared from the outside. Voices drifted through from the adjacent parlor as the butler retrieved their hats and coats.

"This way, William." Sir Martin led them into the room where the butler announced them.

Mr. Notley came to their side. "It is good that you could come, William. Come, I would like you to meet my wife."

William glanced around the room where several

gentlemen and ladies were gathered. Mr. Notley stopped in front of a handsome, full figured mature lady who appeared younger than her years.

"William," she replied, just as informal as her husband, "it is good to meet you finally." Her warm voice dripped with comfort.

Strange, these people knew him, yet he hardly knew of their existence. His father had not talked about his younger years. Sir George always spent most of his time in London, working in the House of Parliament.

"I am told you are friends with my niece, Eliza," Mrs. Notley spoke.

"Yes," William replied, "we grew up together. She is friends with my sister Abby."

"Eliza is in the other room there." Mrs. Notley indicated an archway which led to another room just off the parlor. "You must let her know you are here. She will be happy to introduce you to her friends."

Eliza's aunt reminded him of his Aunt Lucy. Eliza's familiar laugh could be heard as he moved toward the next room. Several gentlemen conversed, and a group played cards in a corner, lively bantering amongst themselves. Eliza's laughter brought his attention back to the card game. Her laugh resonated. "Eliza?" She looked up. He had not intended to speak out loud.

Her eyes grew wide as recognition dawned. "William." Eliza rose from the table and coming around the side, she reached for him. "When did you get to Bristol? I wasn't expecting you." Her eyes sparkled.

His gaze met hers, and his heart turned over in response. "I came to meet your uncle and finish some business. I see that Bristol has been good for you." His glance traveled the length of her. She grinned then giggled. She was a vision. Appreciation filled William as he watched her in wonder. What had happened to her in the last month since she had been here? It was not just the clothes that framed her to perfection. She glowed with confidence. He realized how much he had missed her.

A cough sounded. Eliza turned. "Oh," she whispered. Her friends had been watching them with curious glances.

"I would like to introduce you to my friends. Miss Dalton, this is William Phelips, the friend from home that I told you about."

"Miss Dalton," William nodded, "I hope she has been kind to me."

Miss Dalton smiled. Cocking her head to one side, she nodded reassurance. "Yes, Eliza has only told me the best of things about you and your sister."

"Mr. Templeton and Mr. Dowding," Eliza replied. "They have been kind enough to escort me around town as I have become familiar with the city." She smiled innocently, apparently unaware of how this information affected him.

Both gentlemen nodded politely but did not attempt to engage him in any further conversation. Eliza excused them and walked around the room making introductions. Everyone was cordial, polite, and treated him with respect. Eliza continued her witty conversations with the gentlemen and ladies he met.

"William." Mr. Notley came up from behind. "Eliza, I am going to steal your friend for a moment."

"How long are you staying in Bristol?" Mr. Notley asked as they walked away.

"I have not decided." William watched Eliza out of the corner of his eye. "I am paid up for a week at the coaching inn."

"Coaching inn," Mr. Notley exclaimed. "No, son of Sir George is going to stay at a coaching inn, not while we are here." He turned and motioned to his wife.

"Mrs. Notley, William, is going to stay with us while he is in town. Would you have the housekeeper get a room ready?"

"William, it will be so nice to have you here. You shall certainly liven up the house." She scurried off in search of the housekeeper.

Mr. Notley chuckled. "It is great to have you here, William, but do not let my wife fool you. She keeps plenty of company here. Not a day goes by that she is not entertaining someone."

"I thank you for your hospitality, Mr. Notley. I will have my valet pack my things and bring them over in the morning."

What luck, William thought, now he could see what Eliza had been up to. He relaxed and settled in to enjoy the rest of the evening.

Eliza kept an eye on William as he talked with her uncle even as she was careful to keep her attention on the young gentlemen vying for her attention. She was starting to feel comfortable in their company. But Eliza was not naïve. She knew they hoped to acquire her uncle's good graces.

She had not expected to see William in Bristol, but she knew she had surprised him. She could tell when he saw her, he looked taken back. It was time he saw her as a grown woman, not the young girl that used to follow him around the meadow.

"Gentlemen, may I steal Miss Grant for a time?" Isabella asked.

Excusing herself, Eliza let Isabella guide her away.

"It is getting harder to get you alone," Isabella commented. "These parties of your aunt's are always so crowded with gentlemen, and you are becoming more popular."

Eliza's laugh rang across the room. She lowered her voice to a whisper. "Yes, Isabella, a rich uncle, and a sizable dowry will do that."

Isabella clicked her tongue. "Men. All they think about is business and money."

"Or horses," Eliza chuckled.

Isabella glanced over at William. "Your friend, William, seems happy to see you. Surely he is not like the other gentlemen here?"

"He is a dear friend, but I fear he is here to check out my uncle's business as well. They will be investing in the next voyage to America, along with a few of his friends."

"They?" Isabella asked.

"Sir Martin introduced my uncle's investment opportunities to William and his friends, Lord Malmesbury and Captain Rutley. That's where I first met Sir Martin."

"I hope he has time for you to show him around Bristol."

"That depends how busy my uncle keeps him." Eliza did not know how long William would be visiting, but she hoped she could show him the town. Maybe he would appreciate her in a new setting where he could see that she was more than his childhood friend.

CHAPTER TWELVE

William adjusted his cravat, checking his reflection in the mirror. Mr. Notley had invited him to breakfast at his Gentleman's club. He had given his valet instructions to pack and move their things into the Notley's home.

"William, I am glad you could come," Mr. Notley extended his hand to William. "You will find us quite informal here. Did you get your things settled at the house?"

"Yes, thank you. My man is settling things this morning. I have been quite impressed with Bristol so far. I had no idea it was such a teeming merchant community."

"Yes, we have done well here over the years. Although the war with France slowed down the commerce, a lot of local merchants are recovering now that the war is over. Mrs. Notley and I have been blessed to weather through the war."

William's father respected this man. "How do you know my father?"

"I met him after Helena and I were married. Sir George was friends with Helena's father. He gave us a loan for our first ship. It gave us the capital to start our business. We have always traded in commodities, never human cargo. Mrs. Notley would have nothing to do with that. I always take supplies with me and bring back raw materials."

"Sir Martin tells me tobacco and cocoa are the main manufacturing commodities for Bristol."

"Yes," Mr. Notley agreed, "Bristol's been processing tobacco for generations as well as cocoa. Liverpool competes for the cotton as their port is larger. But I like to add bales of cotton to the cargo when I have room for the local mills."

Mr. Notley had given William a lot to think about. He agreed with his father that it would be a good investment, especially since the war with France was over. The risk of ships being detained was minimal. Although his tenants and farms were in good shape, more and more of the young men from the village were leaving to work in the cities where they could find jobs and earn higher wages to help support their families. The time would come when their income would fall short as their farms began to vacate. The change was inevitable; it would be wise to prepare.

It was mid-afternoon by the time William finished with Eliza's uncle at the club. He caught a hackney back to their home, and Mr. Notley went to his office.

The butler met William as he entered the house. "My lord, your room is ready. If you will follow me."

"Is Miss Grant in?"

"Yes, my lord, Miss Grant is in the garden picking flowers for tonight's dinner."

He freshened up quickly. He had not been able to talk to Eliza without a bevy of people around last evening. He was anxious to show her his feelings went beyond friendship. What if Eliza rejected him? There was no turning back from this. Was he ready to take the risk? It could ruin the friendship they had shared all his life.

William had a startlingly vivid mental image of Eliza's face tipped toward his, of the way she felt in his arms. Regardless of how brief, it felt natural. He thought he'd like to kiss her. A stupid, ridiculous temptation, but there it was. It had swept over him like a wave, not a ripple but a tidal wave.

Eliza and Isabella went to town that morning, accompanied by their maids and assisted by a driver, while Aunt Helena was busy preparing for her weekly card party that evening.

"I never tire of going to the city. There is so much to

see here. If I were to live here a year, I do not know that I could see it all," Eliza told Isabella.

"I am so glad you are here as well. I am usually accompanied by my stuffy brother, who complains mightily at taking me to town. My mother is always too busy with other things to bother."

"Do you have other siblings?"

"No," Isabella sighed, "I would have liked to have a sister, but it is just my brother and myself."

"I have but one sister, Joanne, but no brothers, although William is like a brother."

"I would have liked to have grown up in the country. Did you have much freedom? Here in the city, I am always escorted by my brother or father. I feel like I cannot spread my wings. There are so many rules."

"There are rules in the country as well, mostly mundane things, that are expected from society, especially for one of our class. But yes, there is freedom too. My sister and I would visit parishioners. I could take a walk or read a book in the open and not be accosted by anyone. The neighbors look out for each other."

Isabella's fingers fumbled with the ribbon on her dress. "William seemed very happy to see you yesterday."

Eliza thought of William, and her heart warmed. "Yes, I was happy to see him too. What about you, Isabella? Do you have someone you are partial to?"

Isabella shook her head. "No, I have no one."

"Will this be your first Season in Bath?"

Isabella's eyes widened. "Oh, no, this will be my third Season. I was eighteen when I had my first."

Stunned, Eliza tried not to show her surprise. "Surely you would have met someone. You are so pretty. I am sure you had gentlemen clamoring for your attention."

"Oh, but I am quite ordinary, not as beautiful as you, Eliza."

Eliza could not believe this. She was astounded that Isabella did not know how attractive she was. Eliza watched Isabella out of the corner of her eye. Isabella was not modest, for she truly believed what she was saying.

Isabella blushed. "I have had plenty of gentlemen single me out. But my brother always warns them off. I believe my mother has certain expectations of the gentleman I will marry."

"What about you, Isabella? What type of gentleman would you like to marry?"

"Well, I should like to love him, and I would hope that he loves me too." Isabella smiled. "And it would be nice if he lived in the country, far away from my parents."

They looked at each other, both bursting into giggles. Eliza could understand her feelings. She was beginning to see how fortunate she was.

Eliza and Isabella finished their shopping just before luncheon. She walked into her aunt's home after leaving Isabella and her maid at her home, promising to pair with each other in a game of whist later that evening.

"Aunt Helena, is there anything I can do to help?"

Aunt Helena looked up from her duties as she instructed the maids. "Oh, Eliza, you're back. Yes, dear, could you gather some flowers from the garden and make some arrangements for our dinner table this evening? There are vases set up in the cold room."

Eliza loved to arrange flowers. She took off her bonnet and went to her room to change to an older gown, tied on an old apron and grabbed the old straw hat she liked to wear. Armed with a basket and scissors, she walked to the garden, her heart lifting.

William exited the back door and walked through the garden, looking for his intended target. He found her bent over a clutch of asters, an old straw hat concealing her curls. His heart did an odd maneuver, flipping in his chest.

He plucked a Brown-Eyed Susan and twirled it in between his fingers as he approached, intending to tickle Eliza with it. Soft brown curls fell from beneath the hat. The crunch of gravel beneath his feet startled her, and she swung around, placing her hand over her heart.

Eliza let out a breath, and her eyes softened around the edges as they met his. "William, you startled me." Her green eyes took on a new hue in the sun.

Handing her the flower, he swept up her basket and hung it on his arm. "I have come out to help you."

She looked around the garden, eyeing him with suspicion. "Where did you come from?"

"I just returned from having breakfast with your uncle at his club. I have been invited to stay here while in town. I understand you are arranging flowers for dinner tonight." William bowed, holding tight to the basket, so the flowers did not spill. "I am here to serve you." He grinned.

Eliza's brow wrinkled, then it cleared. "Fine. Follow me." She started cutting flowers, leaves, and other greenery. He didn't really know what the names were, but he followed dutifully as the basket filled, resisting the urge to tease. They continued into the cold room where vases were set out on sheets of paper laid out along the table.

Eliza observed him, "I am making arrangements for tonight's party, are you sure you want to help? It will be rather dull?"

"Of course. Don't you want me to help?" William didn't care if it was dull, as long as he was with her, a perk of being a childhood friend.

"Well, yes, it is nice having you here," She relaxed, her smile increasing his heart rate. "What I need you to do is to sort the flowers out by color and leave them in piles." She showed him how to lay the flowers neatly on the white paper, then she arranged the greenery, so they were in groups alongside the flowers, each variety having its own stack.

She stood back, her hands on her hips. A sweet smile on her lips. "Do you think you can do that for me?" A challenge in her eyes.

He shook his head. "Do you think me so daft that I cannot arrange stacks of flowers?" He cocked his head and chuckled. Picking up the flowers, he sorted them, doing just as Eliza had demonstrated.

Eliza left the room, bringing back an arm full of vases. She inspected his work. "Not bad." She gave him a teasing glance.

William leaned back against the bench as he watched Eliza take a single flower and, one by one, turn them into colourful bouquets.

"I didn't know you could arrange flowers?"

"Who do you think has been arranging all those flowers you see at church we attend on Sundays?" She smiled as she tickled his nose with the end of a stray bloom.

He resisted a sneeze and instead grabbed her hand, extracting the stem. Rubbing his thumb across her knuckles, he held on longer than was necessary before letting her hand slide from his grasp.

Eliza dimpled and lowered her head. "I think we are

done here. I'll let Aunt Helena know the arrangements are ready." She slid past him and slipped from the room. William liked the feel of her hand in his. She hadn't resisted his touch. William wondered what she was thinking as he watched her retreat.

Eliza ducked out of the cold room as quickly as she could. Uncomfortable with the feelings William had invoked in her, she had used her aunt as an excuse to leave. Although she was glad William was visiting, it would be hard seeing him every day. This softer side of him was unsettling.

"Aunt Helena, the arrangements are ready. I've left them in the cold room. Is there anything else I can do for you?"

Her aunt looked around, a finger on her cheek. "I think I have everything in hand, Eliza, thank you. Why not take some time and relax a little before the guests arrive? I know it has been a busy month for you."

Eliza took advantage of the quiet time and went into the library in search of some reading material. Her aunt was correct. She had been busy since she arrived in Bristol, there had been little time to relax. It was also an excuse to flee the company of William because she couldn't trust herself, especially when he held her hand.

Eliza ran her hand along the rows of books. It was

an impressive library, grander than the vicarage, but smaller than Lord Malmesbury's. Most of the titles were about shipping, navigation, and business. She found a few novels that looked interesting. Pulling one from the shelf, she settled in a chair and began to read.

CHAPTER THIRTEEN

William searched the house when Eliza hadn't returned. She seemed to have disappeared after leaving him. Maybe she retired, resting until the party this evening. William made his way to the library. The Notley's library was smaller than his father's. He scanned the room as his eyes adjusted to the lighting. A miniature ship stood on the mantel. His gaze swept the room and found Eliza nodding in a chair, a book on her lap, fingers grazing the page.

He settled himself in the opposite chair and admired her relaxed countenance, which made her more beautiful than ever. She stirred. Realizing Eliza would not appreciate him watching her sleep, he reached over and gently closed the book. Her eyes fluttered. She yawned and stretched. Her eyes blinked, coming into focus staring into William's eyes. She gave her head a slight shake. "William, how long have you been sitting there?" her voice accusatory.

"Just a few minutes." Unaffected by her tone, he continued to gaze into her warm brown eyes. "I thought I would come and retrieve a book and here you were, sleeping. Your book was not interesting?" He chuckled.

She looked at the book in her lap and shifted her weight. "No, I'm just tired. Since I have been here, my aunt and uncle have been hosting company several nights a week. I am not used to the late nights they kept here in the city. Tonight is my aunt's whist party. She never misses a week." Eliza yawned. "Isabella has agreed to partner with me, I am getting rather good at it."

"Guests seem to talk about business quite a lot with your uncle."

"You have noticed. I think most of the guests come for an excuse to talk business with Uncle Notley."

Hardly, he suspected some had come for other reasons. "What about Mr. Dowding and Mr. Templeton?" An*d Sir Martin*, he remembered the attention the gentleman gave Eliza while in Somerset.

Her brow wrinkled.

"Abby told me in one of your letters, you mentioned spending time with them, I noticed they were at the party the other night." William focused on her face waiting for a reaction.

Eliza's mouth dropped open, then closed. She laughed softly, smiling. That smile made his insides tickle, right down to his boots, then working its way back up to flutter around his ribcage somewhere. Most disconcerting.

"Oh, Mr. Dowding and Mr. Templeton." Her voice rose an octave. "Yes, they do spend quite a bit of time here. They are quite nice and very attentive." Eliza giggled, biting her lip.

William did not like the sound of that. She was teasing, right? He wondered if they were vying to court her. He would keep an eye on those two. Maybe put a bug in their ear. Something uncomfortable settled in his stomach, and he did not like the feeling.

Not one bit.

Eliza looked at the mantel. The clock showed half-past four. "Oh, my. I must get ready. Please excuse me." She stood, and before he knew it, she had left.

Dissatisfaction settled over him. It was worse than he figured.

Slamming his fists on the arms of the chair. No one was going to court Eliza. He would keep her so busy she would have no time to spend with anyone else.

Eliza closed the library door and returned to her bedchamber. What was it that she had written to Abby in her letters, and why would she tell William about it? Why would William care about her gentleman callers? His face had gone dark at the mention of them. He was just being protective, like an older brother. She didn't need William to be a brother.

Eliza wore one of her most delicate gowns for the evening. Aunt Helena had been very generous with her new wardrobe. *A girl should look her best to capture a husband*, her aunt had explained. With no daughters to fawn over, her aunt had lavished Eliza with so many dresses and accessories she felt like a princess. Would William notice?

Eliza's aunt and uncle stood in the foyer, welcoming the guests and introducing William, whom they kept by their side. Eliza helped with the younger crowd. The card tables sat in the parlor, ready for the games to begin.

"Eliza." Isabella moved to her side, concern showing on her face. "My mother and father are here tonight, and they want to meet your friend, William."

Eliza followed Isabella's line of sight where her aunt and uncle were talking to Isabella's parents. Isabella's brother followed behind, looking bored, as usual. Maybe William would become Benjamin's friend. He looked like he needed one.

"Isabella, why does your brother come to these parties when he seems so bored most of the time?" She'd noticed Benjamin was bad-humored and sometimes downright rude. The whole time she'd been acquainted with him, he had never shown any enthusiasm.

"Mother wants him here, so he comes to please her."

Isabella absently scrunched a piece of her skirt in her hand. "I hope they don't say something to embarrass me." She released her gown and tried to smooth the wrinkles.

What would William think of them? Eliza thought Isabella's parents were rather proud and indifferent to Isabella. Benjamin acted the same. For that matter, Isabella's brother had never paid much attention to her, either.

"Most of you have been here before," Aunt Helena explained. "Choose your partners, and we will play two rounds for thirty minutes each. The standard rules of whist apply as put down by Edmond Hoyle. None of those silly variations that are becoming so popular will be allowed. I take the game very seriously." She smiled knowingly as laughter filled the room.

Eliza and Isabella settled down at their table. William approached with Mr. Templeton. "Mr. Templeton has agreed to partner with me, ladies." He nodded as they joined their table, sitting opposite Templeton. Isabella shuffled the cards then invited William to cut the deck. Her slim fingers dealt the cards with much dexterity. Eliza gathered her cards in her hand, her mouth forming a line, satisfied with the hand she'd been dealt.

∼

William studied his cards as Miss Dalton dealt them to each player. He snuck a look at Eliza. She was very alluring tonight, and it wasn't just because of her gown. Her face had a bloom of color that added to her radiance. A strand of hair slipped from her pins, touching her cheek. He was tempted to finger it, if he could. Silky and soft-looking, it was absolutely beautiful with just a hint of gold he hadn't noticed before.

Templeton coughed. "Your turn," he looked at William.

Eliza and Miss Dalton played well together. Almost as if they could tell what the other was about to do. They had apparently partnered many times. William leaned back in his chair as Templeton tallied up the last hand.

Eliza perked up. "It seems we have won, gentlemen." She peered over, looking at the points Templeton had totaled.

Mr. Templeton laid the cards aside. "Yes, you two win again, Miss Grant." He laughed good-naturedly.

"We do make a good team." Her nose crinkled, smiling at Miss Dalton.

Guests rose and began to mingle as the first round ended. William bowed to Templeton. "See you at the next table." He walked over to the refreshment table, retrieving a drink from a servant.

"I am told you have an estate in Somerset County?" Mrs. Dalton inquired.

William turned and found himself wedged between

Miss Dalton's parents. Mrs. Dalton looked nothing like her daughter. Her gray somber eyes drilled into him. Although well-dressed, her manners were direct.

"Yes, the family seat of Montacute sits in Somerset County." William nodded politely.

Before William could blink, they were discussing his father's holdings and properties. He was finding it difficult to extract himself, his head reeling at the amount of information they were able to gather. He backed away, just to have Mrs. Dalton place her pale hand on his arm, asking another question, drawing him back like vultures devouring its prey. He was being picked to pieces.

"Mr. Dalton, Mrs. Dalton, it's time for the next round of whist. I have come to claim my partner," Mr. Templeton broke into the conversation.

William was never so grateful for an interruption.

"I feel like I have just been fleeced."

"Yes. I find it best to stay clear of the Daltons if I can," Mr. Templeton agreed.

William and Templeton joined another table as the next round of whist began. They managed to win a few rounds by the end of the evening.

Templeton offered his hand as the tables broke up. "Thank you. We did manage to win a few by the end of the evening." He chuckled. "Mrs. Notley is serious about her whist, but I only come out of respect for Mr. Notley."

"You do business together?" William asked.

"I am hoping to invest in the next voyage. And you? Sir Martin mentioned you visited the ships."

"I am here to invest in the next voyage as well. My father, Sir George Phelips, has only good things to say about Mr. Notley. I wanted to come and see the operation for myself." William and Templeton moved toward the buffet.

William filled a plate from the cold supper laid out on the table.

"Mr. Phelips," Isabella spoke softly over his shoulder.

"Miss Dalton." William turned, and a nervous look crossed her face.

"I do not mean to be so bold," Isabella said, "but I hope my parent's did not bother you in any way?" She nibbled on her bottom lip as she glanced in her parent's direction.

"Nothing I cannot handle, Miss Dalton." He could not blame her for her parents uncouth behavior.

"It is just that—" She blushed.

He felt a flash of sympathy for her. "I do not fault you in any way for their behavior," William assured her. "Eliza has only good things to say about your friendship."

Miss Dalton visibly relaxed. "I am glad to hear about it. I like Miss Grant very much." She dimpled as she met his eyes.

Miss Dalton was charming, but she didn't make his

insides tickle as Eliza did. It was apparent she was embarrassed by her parents' behavior.

"I suspect you have come to Bristol for more than business with Mr. Notley." Isabella's look shifted across the room.

William followed her gaze and met Eliza's, whose pretty hazel eyes were watching them. He nodded and smiled before turning his attention back to Miss Dalton.

"Is it really so obvious?"

"Not to others maybe, but Miss Grant speaks very highly of you, and I watched her when you first arrived," she explained. "There are little things that a woman would notice."

"I shall have to be more careful in your presence," he laughed. "You remind me of my sister Abby, Miss Dalton. I think you would like each other. I hope we can be friends."

"I would like that," Miss Dalton replied, her voice brightening. "I have heard all about your sister from Miss Grant. I would like to meet her someday."

"Eliza has written about you to Abby as well. She read me one of her letters and mentioned she would like to meet you. You should write her and introduce yourself. I could give you the address?"

"I would like that, thank you Mr. Phelips."

William again joined Mr. Notley at his club for breakfast. It had been a restless night, worrying about Eliza. A plan had formed during the early hours of the morning just before he finally had fallen asleep. He had conceived a way to knock his competition out of the running. He would start his campaign immediately.

Sir Martin had entered the main hall where comfortable chairs were scattered around inviting conversation. The dining room veered off to the left. Since William had been in Bristol, Sir Martin had not paid any particular attention to Eliza and Templeton seemed only concerned with business.

William noticed Mr. Dowding conversing with three gentlemen across the room so he approached. "Mr. Dowding. May I have a private conversation with you?"

Dowding blinked, giving William a nod. He broke off from the group and walked a few paces away, joining William in a private corner.

"What can I help you with, sir?"

"Last night I found you quite attentive, to the ladies. As you know Miss Grant and I are old friends. We grew up together in Somerset County. I feel somewhat responsible for her, given the fact that her father is not in town."

Dowding listened, his brow creasing.

"I feel almost like a brother to Miss Grant," William continued. "Are you a God-fearing man Mr. Dowding? I ask because Miss Grant's father is the vicar in our parish."

"Yes, I go to church regularly, when I can." The gentleman stumbled on his words.

"It is only that I noticed you and Miss Grant have been on friendly terms in the week that I have been here."

"Yes," Mr. Dowding replied. "Her uncle and I do business together. I try to stay on friendly terms."

"Let me be frank, Mr. Dowding, What are your intentions towards Miss Grant?"

"My intentions?" The confusion was written on his face.

"I only ask for her father's sake, being he is not here to judge your character himself. Miss Grant does have a small dowry, and I would like to make sure any gentleman courting her is of a good character," William explained. "One worthy of a vicar's daughter."

"Courting her?" The poor man's confusion turned to astonishment.

Mr. Dowding stuttered, "On my honor sir, I have never given Miss Grant any reason to believe there was an understanding between us. I have only given her the utmost courtesy due to the niece of Mr. Notley."

William studied Mr. Dowding, nodding. He was relieved he was wrong. "So, it seems I have misjudged your friendliness toward Miss Grant. I do apologize." William bowed. He couldn't help but egg him a little.

William gave him a sheepish smile as he cleared his throat then lowered his voice. "Mr. Dowding, forget

what I have said and we shall keep this just between
us."

"Certainly, sir. This will go no further. And I
promise to be more careful in the future. I would not
want to give false hope." Dowding bowed and took his
leave, apparently eager to be away.

He feared he played it a little thick but admitted
enjoying his little farce. William vowed to keep Eliza so
busy that no other gentleman would have time to spend
with her. He was prepared to follow her to Bath if
need be.

CHAPTER FOURTEEN

*E*liza slept late in the morning, having put in a late night. Usually, she would excuse herself and retire earlier from these parties. The guests varied depending on whom her uncle was entertaining, but their regular friends were often in attendance and that included the Daltons, which allowed her to see more of Isabella.

William's presence caused her to stay up later. He and Isabella, it seemed, had become... acquainted. They had talked quite often throughout the evening, and by Isabella's animated expressions, she could tell her new friend liked William and William seemed to like her as well which gave Eliza unsettled feelings.

Her aunt was alone when Eliza entered the breakfast parlor. "William left with your uncle earlier this morning to breakfast at his gentlemen's club. A note arrived this morning." Her aunt nodded to an envelope on the table beside her.

Eliza let out a breath as she sat down. Ramsey poured her coffee. She leaned back letting her head clear from the late night before, or rather, the early morning. Opening the letter, she began reading as she sipped the hot drink.

"Mr. Dowding has sent word that he cannot make it for our drive today." Eliza put down her cup. "The weather is sunny. I was so looking forward to a morning drive."

"My dear, why should you stay home? I'll order the buggy and have Ramsey put extra bricks for warmth to rest your feet on. Ruby can accompany you." Aunt Notley waved her hand.

Splendid, she would enjoy the afternoon after all.

Eliza hurried to change after breakfast and inform Ruby of the change in plans.

Eliza was settled with Rudy by her side. She drove into the lane and headed toward the park at a sedate pace, proper for a young lady, she reminded herself. She resisted the urge to move faster. She could let the horse have his head once they made it into the park.

She had gotten very adept at handling the buggy and loved the feel of the wind and sense of freedom it gave her, reminding her of home. Eliza picked up speed as they made it onto the gravel road just inside the park finally racing around the track at a pretty good clip, careful not to infringe on anyone's space.

Ruby clutched the side of the buggy, her other hand grasping her bonnet, eyes wide. Eliza had added a few extra hat pins to her bonnet before leaving home. After one round through the park, she slowed the buggy for her maid's sake and to not overtax the horse.

"Ruby, do you not like to go fast?" Eliza teased as she took a breath, her cheeks felt chilled. She let the reins loosen through her gloved fingers.

"I would not say I do, miss."

Eliza laughed. "This reminds me of back home in the country. I love the park and its wide green expanses."

"Yes, miss," her maid's hand was still gripping the rail of the buggy.

"I promise to go slower for the rest of the trip." Eliza gave her maid a reassuring smile.

Eliza noticed Mr. Dowding coming towards them on his mount. She caught his eye and smiled, ready to give a friendly greeting. He startled when seeing her. Recovering, he gave her a quick nod and turned his mount in the other direction.

That was strange, Eliza thought, turning around to see if anyone was behind her, but the path was clear. Mr. Dowding usually stopped and greeted her. He was usually very cordial each time they met. Was he feeling guilty at canceling their ride this morning? Eliza shrugged as she maneuvered the buggy out of the park and onto the main thoroughfare. By the time they made it back to her aunt's home, her cheeks were flushed from the cold weather, but she felt invigorated.

Eliza sat in the parlor with her aunt when William returned home. He felt he had made good progress in his plans.

"Eliza, your uncle has offered his tickets at the theater tonight. Would you like to accompany me? We could invite Miss Dalton and her brother," William suggested.

"May I, Aunt Helena?"

"Yes, dear, your uncle has box seats at the theater and we rarely go unless he wants to entertain associates and their wives. You go and have a nice time with your friends." Her aunt smiled.

"Thank you, William. I would love to go to the theater."

"Excellent. I will send an invitation to Miss Dalton and her brother." William turned leaving the room, eager to get the invitation sent off.

One less evening spent around her uncle's stodgy cohorts. William would enlist Miss Dalton's aid in his courtship with Eliza. She had been his friend for so long he feared she would resist his advances as a suitor. He would need to be strategic to win her heart. Would she see him in a new light, a suitor rather than a friend? He was thankful he had brought his own vehicle to town. It would be tight but the four of them would just fit and Eliza would be tucked up next to him.

He'd received word that the Daltons would expect them at seven.

William's heart rate increased at the sight of Eliza coming down the stairs. A shy smile touched her lips. Stepping forward, he took the cloak from her arm as she descended the last stair. She turned her back, and he wrapped her cloak around her shoulders. Closing his eyes, he caught her scent, breathing her in. He resisted burying his nose in her hair and pulling her into an embrace, tucking her hand into his arm instead. He could feel warmth through her gloved hand, giving him a warm, cozy feeling. The feeling he was home.

"You look lovely, Eliza," William spoke, his voice husky even to his ears.

There he said it. He pulled Eliza closer to his side and waited for her reply.

Her eyes widened as she looked into his face. "Thank you, William," she smiled. "You look very nice too." She blushed. Reaching her hand to her neck, she pulled the fur-lined hood tight around her face as they stepped into the cold.

William helped her into the carriage and then tucked

a blanket around her tightly, protecting her like the precious package she was.

Eliza sighed, then giggled. "What?" he asked.

"I cannot believe the change in you, William. You have yet to tease me once since you have been in town."

"I am affronted. I promised you that I would not tease you anymore, and I would treat you like a lady." He feigned hurt until his smile broke through.

She laughed with him. "Do you know, Abby and I were tempted to wager that you wouldn't be able to do it," Eliza admitted.

"Do what?"

"To stop teasing." She nudged him playfully. "Although I admit I do miss it sometimes."

"Ha, well, you should have more faith in me."

The carriage stopped in front of a modest townhouse. William jumped out, leaving Eliza tucked warmly in the blankets. He walked to the door.

After making small talk with Isabella's parents, he escorted her out the front door. Benjamin hurried to the carriage, climbing in with no regard to helping his sister causing William to cringe. He retrieved another blanket from under the seat handing it to Benjamin who sat next to Eliza. Retrieving the blanket, he laid it across his lap.

William's eyes found Eliza's, and she gave him a shrug. He helped Miss Dalton into the carriage and joined her on the same seat. William made small talk while trying to curb his frustration with Benjamin. Try as he might, he could not like the fellow.

Eliza smiled to herself as she watched William trying to contain his frustration with Benjamin. She had known William long enough to know when he was irritated.

"Isabella, I am so happy you could come to the theater with us," Eliza commented. "I have not been since coming to town and am so excited."

Isabella smiled. "I haven't been before either, we shall enjoy our first time together." Her laughter rang out as they chatted.

Eliza glanced at Benjamin every so often. He had settled back against the seat, his eyes closed saying not a word throughout the journey. Her hopes that the two would become friends was fading. She could understand William's frustration with Benjamin's behavior. But she had grown used to it in the weeks she had been here. She was thankful Isabella was here and that her brother agreed to escort her.

They edged their way through the crowded theater, entering their box with a prime view of the stage. Benjamin sat behind her, leaving William to sit beside Isabella.

The curtain rose, and the play began. Eliza became engrossed in the scenes before her, sometimes laughing, sometimes with a tear coming to her eye. The curtain came down, signaling intermission. She felt awed. "That was wonderful."

"Ladies, may I get you some refreshment?" William asked.

"Thank you, that would be nice." Eliza turned to find Benjamin was no longer behind her. "When did your brother leave?"

Isabella waved her hand. "Do not worry about Benjamin," Isabella spoke softly. "He is always disappearing. He only came because my mother insisted he escort me. I am just glad he agreed to come with me tonight. I would have hated to miss the play."

"What do you think of the play so far?" Eliza asked.

"I love it."

William came back into the booth, juggling three glasses of punch.

"Thank you." Isabella gently took one of the glasses from William's hand.

William handed a glass to Eliza before sitting next to her.

A knock sounded at the door, and a couple came in, beginning a line of introductions. Eliza retrieved his drink from his hand as curious people wanted to be introduced to him — only dispersing as the second act began.

"You are quite popular tonight," Eliza whispered, handing him his glass of punch before turning her attention to the play. She watched him with a sidelong glance. He sipped his drink, his eyes appearing glazed.

He was popular. It was his easy way with people. She could see the mothers lining up to push their daughters in front of him now that they had an introduction.

William was glad that Eliza and Isabella were enjoying the play. He never much liked them. He had been to a few productions while in London, mainly as an escort for his sister. Going to the theater was an excuse to be seen by their neighbors, and it didn't appear to be much different here in Bristol.

Benjamin had slipped out before the end of the first act, never bothering to show up again. He was surprised at his indifference to his sister, but he let it pass. It was more pleasant without him brooding in the background, pushing his way into Eliza's space.

Eliza and Isabella excused themselves to the retiring room while William waited, conversing with some new acquaintances. Isabella's brother still hadn't shown his face when Isabella returned.

"I do apologize for my brother," Isabella remarked as she looked among the crowds.

William held his tongue, preferring not to embarrass Miss Dalton any more than she already was.

"I would like to say this is unusual behavior for him. But... he only escorted me because of my parents' insistence. I fear what you must think of us." Isabella flushed.

"Do not trouble yourself, Miss Dalton. I do not measure you by your brother's behavior. I only wonder," William reassured her. "My sister, Abby would certainly take me to task were I to put her in a similar situation."

"You are too kind." She hesitated as a slight blush pinked in her cheeks. William waited for her to speak further. She looked around the room, obviously nervous. "I only speak this because we have agreed to be friends, and I would hate to have further embarrassment laid upon you."

"Continue, Miss Dalton. Do not be afraid to speak your mind. I will not be offended, I promise," William reassured her.

"It's just that my parents have hopes that you and I…" She blushed more deeply. "That is why they are allowing me to spend time with you and Eliza."

William admitted this astonished him. He wasn't used to being the object of designing parents, although he had seen plenty of it in London. William could see that Miss Dalton was embarrassed to admit this to him and he liked her better for it.

"I understand, it happens more than you may think. Especially in London." He smiled, leaning in as he whispered, "We shall keep this our secret, and you may continue to spend time with Eliza."

Miss Dalton relaxed. "Eliza is lucky to have you. Thank you for understanding."

He looked up to see Eliza approaching. "It seems

Benjamin has disappeared." William informed her. "Shall we dine without him?"

Eliza's brow crinkled as she looked to Isabella.

Isabella smiled. "I think that will be lovely. Don't worry, Eliza. My brother can take care of himself."

William offered both ladies an arm as they exited the theater.

CHAPTER FIFTEEN

*E*liza woke early the next morning even after the late evening the night before. She had seen William and Isabella as she left the withdrawing room last evening. William's head bent over listening to Isabella speak. Her stomach had done a somersault as she watched Isabella blush, and William smiling. His eyes had lit when she approached. That Benjamin had disappeared had not surprised her. The evening was lovely just the same.

She had the urge to take a turn around the park with her aunt's gig and asked Ramsey if the grooms could have it ready for a morning ride. She hurried to the breakfast room, anxious to start her day.

William came through the door as she finished her toast and chocolate. His hair glistened, and he smelled of warm spice as he removed his gloves and tapped them on his pant leg.

"I thought I would join you for your ride this morning."

"How did you know I was going for a ride?" Eliza wiped her hands on a napkin then laid it on the table beside her empty plate.

"I had just returned from the club when I noticed the gig being prepared. The grooms informed me that you ride most mornings."

Eliza gave him a sharp look as she moved toward the door. "That will be fine, but I am driving."

He chuckled as he followed her, offering his arm. Eliza eyed him before accepting his escort. He tugged her in closer as he guided her out the door to the waiting gig. Ruby was waiting patiently outside.

"Ruby, William has decided to escort me on my morning ride so you shall be spared today."

"Yes, miss." She curtsied. "My lord." Ruby made her way back to the house.

William assisted Eliza into the gig before settling by her side. His leg nestled against hers, she could feel his warmth beneath her skirts. She glanced sideways. His big frame was a tight squeeze on the small bench seat. Her nimble fingers shook the reins and guided the vehicle out onto the street.

"Why did you say your maid would be spared?"

"Oh, I like to go a little faster than she does." She smiled.

When they approached the park, Eliza gently guided the gig through the gate. Then before approaching the promenade, she turned. "You may want to hold on to your hat," she smiled. Flicking the reins, she urged the horse to go faster.

William gripped the side of the seat and threw his hand to his hat to keep it from flying off as they raced along the promenade, passing riders along the way. She made one pass around the track before slowing the horse to a steady trot. William slacked his grip as the gig slowed. Her eyes flashed, and her cheeks were flush. She had thoroughly enjoyed herself; he thought as his breath evened out.

"Eliza," he chuckled. "I didn't know you enjoyed a fast ride. Where did you learn to drive like that?"

"I have been practicing while in Bristol. My aunt's horse and gig are much finer than ours at home."

He had not known this Eliza existed. Where was the sedate little vicar's daughter? He liked this side of her.

"I like to come in the mornings so I can have a fast ride without the matrons disapproving of me." She watched him while the horse walked at a modest pace. "I have shocked you."

He laughed outright, noticing her bonnet still in place. A few tendrils of hair had come undone, dangling around her face. He wondered what she would look like if she let loose her pins. He resisted the urge to tuck in the stray locks.

"I admit to being a little surprised, but I am not shocked," he assured her.

Eliza pulled back onto the main street. And for the next hour, she took him on a tour, regaling him with a bit of Bristol history. She surprised him again at the knowledge she had acquired in such a short time. They stopped at the coffeehouse on Corn Street for refreshment.

William noticed Mr. Dowding coming their way as they returned to the gig. Mr. Dowding stopped dead on seeing them, ducked his head and crossed the lane.

"That's strange."

"Yes." William crinkled his brow.

"Wasn't that, Mr. Dowding? It has been bizarre this past week. It is almost as if he is avoiding us."

"Who?" William questioned, trying to keep a straight face.

"Mr. Dowding. Didn't you see him? He tipped his hat and walked across the street as if he wanted to avoid us."

"I visited with him just this morning at your uncle's club."

Her frown increased before her eyes widened, "William, are you implying that Mr. Dowding is avoiding *me*?"

"That's ridiculous," William replied, maintaining his composure. "Why would Mr. Dowding avoid you? I thought you were the best of acquaintances." He kept his eyes forward, hoping she wouldn't see through his facade, for if she ever learned of his deed, he feared she might never forgive him.

Eliza was truly puzzled at Mr. Dowding's behavior. Even his friend seemed to be avoiding her when not weeks before they were so attentive. It was enough to make a girl think she had grown a second nose. After a bite to eat, Eliza let William drive them back to her aunt's home. It had been a fun morning. She had enjoyed her time with William, and he had not scolded her for driving fast.

Slowly, one by one, her gentlemen callers had stopped coming, leaving only William to attend her, while the days grew colder as they fell into a routine. William would join her each day for a ride through the park. She found herself reading journals and the tourist pamphlets, studying the history of Bristol so she could give William a commentary on the places they visited.

October blew into November. Eliza knew their outings with her aunt's gig were coming to a close. This last drive would be special, she thought as she dressed warmly. Christmas was coming, and she had planned on spending it at the vicarage with her father and sister before ringing in the new year.

"William, I would like to go to the market today," Eliza said as they finished their breakfast. "I want to buy some gifts for my family."

William, waiting for her in the hall, escorted her to the gig. She watched as he gently tucked blankets around her legs and made sure the bricks were placed just right. She smiled to herself as a warm feeling bubbled up inside. Abby wouldn't recognize her new brother.

"What?" William asked as he slid in beside her. "You have been giving me that mischievous look."

"I have been thinking about how much you have changed from the boy I used to know. I don't think Abby would recognize you." Eliza laughed.

He gave her his teasing smile as he offered her the reins. "Oh, no, William, you drive today." She tossed her head in his direction. "It's much too cold." She tucked her gloved hands into her fur muff.

Eliza, emboldened by his smile, leaned a little closer as they headed onto the lane. The wind picked up as it blew off the coast, adding a chill to the morning breeze.

William maneuvered the gig to the curb alongside the market. Eliza stepped from the gig and William released her hand. The little black boy, who she had seen while shopping with Isabella, popped behind them grabbing the horse's lead.

"I can take good care of your gig, sir. Please?" the little boy pleaded as he looked up at William.

"Well, now," William replied. "You look kind of small for the job. Are you sure you can handle it?"

"Yes, sir, I can. I am older than I look." The small

boy grinned up at William. A perfect row of white teeth gleamed from his mouth.

William moved aside, gathering the reins. "Climb up there on this seat," he instructed. "Go ahead and tuck that blanket around you and put your toes on that brick. Now, make sure that the horse doesn't go anywhere." William placed the reins into the boy's small hands.

"Yes, sir." The boy grinned as he settled his bare toes on the brick and gripped tightly onto the reins.

William flashed a coin in front of the boy. "Now, if you take good care of this horse and gig, I will give you another coin when I get back. Agreed?"

The young boy's eyes followed the coin in William's hand. Shaking his head, he reached for the money. His eyes lit as he bit the coin then stuffed it into his pocket. "Yes, sir. I will take good care of them, sir."

"You're sure he'll be able to handle the gig?" Eliza asked, throwing the boy a concerned glance over her shoulder.

William chuckled, a warm sound to her ears. "We will see, but I think he is man enough to handle it."

Eliza's heart went out to the boy with his bare feet and ragged clothing. Surely his owner could take better care of him? He seemed to run the streets. This wasn't the first time she had seen him scurrying about.

Eliza entered merchant stalls filled with colorful fabrics, ribbons, and many delights, putting the boy to the back of her mind. "Do you think Joanne will like this?" She held a beautiful shawl with a floral print and lace edges for William to see.

"It looks like something Abby would wear," William gazed at the shawl and fingered the edges.

"I will take it." She handed it to the clerk, hoping her sister would love it.

She and William enjoyed a hot drink at the coffeehouse, the cup warming her hands. "I have seen the boy here before. The first time I was with Isabella, he ran past here and hid under our table."

"I have seen many urchins running the street in London."

"I have heard the stories," Eliza said. "I feel something for this one, I cannot explain it." She looked into William's eyes with a shrug of her shoulder.

He reached his hand up then let it drop. "That is because you have a kind soul," William spoke softly. Dropping his eyes, he sipped his coffee before putting the cup down. "We should probably go check on our gig, do you think?"

She nodded, reaching for the packages as William reached at the same time, their fingers colliding. A thrill ran through her and she quickly pulled back. William gathered the packages as she stood.

A terrible noise sounded as they neared the gig. Eliza grew alarmed as she watched the little black boy running around the gig and ducking under the wheel. The deplorable man—presumably his owner, tried to snatch him, a string of oaths coming from his mouth.

"Sir, you will hurt the boy," she yelled as she hurried to the gig.

"You." The man spat as he turned and caught sight of Eliza. "I told you before. I will not be interfered with. The boy is my property." He advanced towards her.

Eliza's temper flared at her concern for the young boy. William stepped in front of her just stopping the advance of the angry man.

"What is the meaning of this?" William stepped forward, shielding her.

"This here boy is my property." The man eyed William. The dirty man backed up a few steps, taking in the cut of William's clothing. "I won't have no abolitionist interfering." He gave Eliza a fierce look.

"We are not trying to interfere with your property. We merely hired the boy to watch our gig." William explained as he pulled a few coins from his pocket. "He's done a fine job." William looked at the boy as Eliza watched with pride at his compassion. "What's your name?" he asked the boy.

"Sam." The young boy squeaked as he peered over the other side of the gig. His eyes widened. He looked between William and his owner.

"Thank you, Sam. You did a fine job." William said, tossing a few coins to the young boy who scurried to gather them up.

"That will be enough," the old man grumbled. "It's time we get home." He grabbed hold of the young boy and made to drag him away.

"May I have your name, sir?"

"My name, what be it to you?" he protested, watching William warily.

"I just want to know the name of Sam's owner."

"Mr. Donnelly. The owner's name is Mr. Donnelly. I am the overseer," he admitted before dragging little Sam off behind him.

Eliza's heart tightened as she watched Sam disappear from sight. "He's probably going to take the money away from him."

"You're probably right." William helped Eliza into the gig. He stowed the packages behind their seat before climbing in and adjusting the reins.

That nasty man had called her an abolitionist.

Again.

CHAPTER SIXTEEN

*T*he small family had just finished dinner, and they were enjoying port in the parlor. William and Sir Martin were present for an unusually quiet evening at home.

"Aunt Helena, what's an abolitionist?"

"Well, dear," her aunt replied. "That's someone who is trying to abolish slavery. We have a few leading abolitionists in town."

"I thought slavery was already banned." Eliza was puzzled.

"New slaves can't be brought in to England, but the ones here are not free," her uncle replied.

"Aren't your butler and housekeeper free?"

"The owners of slaves can free them," her aunt explained.

Eliza's mind churned with the dilemma. Then if she

bought Sam, she could free him. But what would a little boy do without a home? Where would she come up with that kind of money? And who would sell a boy to a woman? It all seemed so unfair. Buying people to work. Back in Somerset, tenants rented the farms from their landowners. If the landowner was fair, the tenant could get ahead in life and send their children to the local school. If not, their oldest son could be educated into a profession.

"You are thinking about Sam, aren't you?" William whispered in her ear.

She jumped. "William, you startled me." Then she laughed at the thought that he always seemed to be doing that.

"Come, let's play a game of chess. Your uncle and Sir Martin are talking about ships again. My eyes are just about to glaze over," he admitted.

Eliza watched as William's nimble fingers set up the chess pieces.

"*Were* you thinking of Sam?" he asked again.

Eliza dimpled. "Yes, I was trying to figure out how I could buy the little boy and then free him." She sighed. "I know it's silly. I have no money, and where would a small boy live once he was freed?" She moved her pawn forward.

"If we were in Somerset, back at Montacute, he could work in the stables. He sure liked the horse."

Eliza gave him a smirk. "What boy doesn't like

horses?" Her fingers brushed against William's as she moved her rook. A jolt ran up her arm as she quickly pulled back. She glanced at him from under her eyelashes. He hadn't seemed to notice.

William's eyes shone as he called checkmate. She sat back enjoying his triumphant grin. What would it be like to kiss those lips? Shocked at where her thoughts were going, she began to set the chess pieces back in place.

"Well, that was easy," William complained. "Usually you are harder to beat." He gave her that smile. She hadn't realized how irresistible it was. Her heart turned to liquid. She had to distance herself from him. Everywhere she turned, he was there making it harder to walk away.

William was eager to find out more information from members of the club about the abolitionists' stand on the Slave Act. He knew his father was legislating new laws in Parliament. If Sir George could introduce a way to free the slaves on British soil... it was worth an attempt. He would need to leave for London to visit his father and present this idea. There had been plenty of men at the club that were willing to support refining of the Slave Act. Mr. Notley had introduced him to several gentlemen at his club who had been writing and giving speeches about the issue. He had learned much through their discussions.

His idea for a gift for Eliza was taking more time than he had anticipated. But if he was successful, he knew it would be the best gift ever. If he could get everything in place before Christmas.

Eliza visited the circulating library with Isabella. The clerk had directed them to the history section.

"This seems a bit dry," Isabella said. "Whatever are you looking for?" She thumbed through a book.

"Do you remember the small black boy that hid under our table in the market that first day we went to the market together?"

Isabella's brow wrinkled. "I believe so."

"A few days ago, William and I visited the market so I could purchase gifts for my family. The little boy watched our gig for us," Eliza explained. "When we returned, his overseer was mistreating him again."

"So, what do you want to find out here?"

"I would like to learn something more. The overseer called me an abolitionist. I want to understand more about the movement."

"You make me ashamed of myself." Isabella fingered the books on a shelf.

Eliza paused, her fingers reaching for a book. "Isabella why would you feel ashamed?"

Isabella ducked her head. "It is just that I have lived in Bristol my whole life. I have never noticed people like you do and the inequality that you speak of," Isabella blushed. "It has only been a short while since slave trading was banned here in Bristol. Before that, I am ashamed to say my family acquired their wealth on the backs of the poor African people. I was never allowed to come to town. The sights were not this pleasant before," Isabella explained. "I hear that slaves are still brought to the West Indies in the Americas."

Eliza felt compassion at her words. "I have heard this too. But surely, Isabella, you have nothing to be ashamed of. You have no control over your family's business dealings any more than I do."

Isabella gave a nervous laugh. "I am afraid I did not give it much thought until you came along and brought it to my attention."

"Well." Eliza sighed pulling some books from the shelf. "I fear I do not have much influence on these matters. But I do like to learn so I don't feel so ignorant on the matter. Perhaps it is because I am a vicar's daughter. I have spent a lot of time visiting the poor parishioners in our county."

"You make me envious," Isabella replied. "My days are spent learning to be a proper lady so that I can fulfill my parents' ambitions."

Eliza and Isabella spent the better part of the morning perusing through dry history books. "We had better leave," Eliza pushed the pile of books away. "My aunt and uncle have a gathering tonight." She stretched her tired muscles before gathering the books to return to the librarian.

Eliza managed to finish a light meal before the party.

"The women's auxiliary of Bristol holds this annual party." Aunt Helena checked Eliza's bow and fluffed her skirt. "You young folks may find it dull, but they have a small orchestra so that the young can dance. It is held in the Great Hall at your uncle's club."

Eliza soon realized what her aunt was preparing her for when they entered the building. Groups of people dressed in their finest were coming in droves. This must be what the balls of the ton were like in London, Eliza thought. Groups of people attending functions to be seen, business deals to be made. Although in London, she imagined it was alliances with families that were being discussed.

The Great Hall had colonnades of pillars along the edges with alcoves of rooms between each. It was impressive. The building could be used for many functions. Eliza scanned the space, looking for a familiar face. How was she to find anyone in this crowd?

She excused herself from her aunt and uncle, who

talked with acquaintances. Skirting the edges of the room, she looked for Isabella or William. Dancers had already formed sets as a small orchestra played music at the top of the room.

"There you are." She turned at the familiar voice behind her. William beamed, his smile glistening in her direction.

"I never thought there would be such a crowd. I have been looking for Isabella."

"They are just over here," William indicated as he escorted her through the crowds. They entered one of the small rooms off the great hall.

A group of young people were gathered talking and mingling amongst each other. Isabella brightened when she saw Eliza.

"I had no idea this party would be so well attended," Eliza said.

"Oh, yes," Isabella replied. "The women's auxiliary is an annual event. You will find most of the business community in attendance."

Eliza's eyes drifted to two ladies hovering behind Isabella.

Isabella took her arm. "Eliza, my friends Miss Gibbs, and Miss Pratt. Miss Grant is Mr. Notley's niece from south Somerset," she informed her friends.

Eliza nodded as Miss Gibb's large sea-green eyes observed her. A sprinkling of freckles dotted her nose and her coppery hair was up in a chignon at the back of her head. She smiled shyly. "Miss Grant."

Miss Pratt had a creamy white complexion. Gray eyes met Eliza's nodding.

"Eliza, may I have this dance?" William interrupted. "Excuse us, ladies." He bowed and led her back through the door into the great hall where a set was just starting.

"Isabella tells me you two spent the afternoon in the circulating library?"

Eliza chuckled. "Yes, we did. It turned out rather a dull day perusing history books all afternoon. I was trying to get more information on the abolitionist movement. I am afraid Isabella found it quite tedious."

The dance started, and Eliza admired William's ability to follow the steps.

"Did you learn anything?" William asked when he faced her again.

"Only that it is a very complicated matter," Eliza replied.

William escorted her back to their friends when the dance ended. "When are you leaving for home?"

"I have written to father and Joanne to expect me in the next few weeks. I am so looking forward to seeing them."

"I have an errand to run. I need to go to London to speak with my father, I should be back in time to escort you home." He gave her a concentrated look. "I have a surprise," he said as he glanced towards Isabella. "I hope you will be pleased, but I shall not tell you until I return," he whispered.

"Miss Dalton, may I have this dance?" William asked Isabella as they joined the small group.

"Most certainly." Isabella took William's arm.

"Mr. Phelips is most handsome," Miss Gibbs whispered to Miss Pratt, who nodded in agreement. "Isabella tells us you are his neighbor." The ladies watched as if Eliza had some great secret to expose.

"I am," Eliza replied. "My father is the vicar of our parish. I have known William all my life."

The ladies twittered in awe as they continued to query her with questions before William and Isabella returned. To their delight, William asked them each to dance, acting the perfect gentleman.

"Your friends seem quite enamored of William."

Isabella laughed. "You know my brother. What gentleman would not shine compared to him? All ladies love the attention of a handsome gentleman."

A little tickle registered in Eliza's middle. William was handsome. Why did it bother her that Isabella stated the fact? He was attentive to the ladies and always had been. It meant nothing in particular, right? William had prospects all around him. The thought didn't reassure her.

Eliza had never been jealous, then why was she feeling so now? She pondered the thought while dancing with several gentlemen watching for a sight of Willian at every turn. She finally excused herself to check on her aunt. She needed a break. Following directions from a footman, she found the retiring room.

"I just know Isabella is going to be able to hook him this week."

Eliza stalled behind the screen, listening to the familiar voice. Slowly, she peeked around the corner. Eliza could just make out Mrs. Dalton talking with a matron who looked to be the same age. She should make herself known, but curiosity stopped her. What was Isabella's mother talking about?

"Mr. Phelips is set to propose soon to Isabella, if she plays her cards right," Mrs. Dalton informed her companion. "He has been meeting with my husband this past week, and I hear he is leaving for London to speak with his father."

"I hear his father is very wealthy," her companion replied.

"He is and Mr. Phelips is the heir. They own a substantial estate in south Somerset. I am so thrilled, Isabella's friendship with Miss Grant has been very profitable."

The Ladies voices faded as they moved from the room. Eliza was stunned. Her head felt light as she struggled to make sense of Mrs. Dalton's conversation. She did not know how long she stood there as the room slowly came back into focus. Was William going to ask for Isabella's hand in marriage? Was he returning to London to inform Sir George? Was that his surprise? The questions churned in her mind. Why was she surprised? Hadn't William told Sir Martin Eliza was just his friend?

Eliza emerged from the retiring room. Her mind going back over the last month. Isabella and William had become friends, she knew that. She didn't know where William spent his time when not with her. Only that William had spent more with her since he arrived in Bristol. Eliza realized it had given her false hope. William must be courting Isabella. Why not, Isabella was fun, friendly, beautiful, and gracious? A perfect wife for William.

Why was the room so hot?

"Miss Grant, are you well?" Sir Martin asked, concern on his face.

Eliza looked up giving Sir Martin a small smile. "I am fine. I was looking for my aunt," she fibbed. She was not fine. Her heart was breaking, no, shattering into a million tiny pieces.

"Come, Miss Grant." Sir Martin took her arm. "I will take you to your aunt. She's just over here."

He did not believe her. She could see by the look in his eyes as he led her to one of the rooms off the great hall. Her aunt was visiting with a group of her peers when they approached. Her aunt's eyes brightened upon seeing Eliza then turned to concern.

"Miss Grant was looking for you, so I escorted her here. I fear she is unwell," Sir Martin whispered.

"Thank you, Sir Martin. Eliza, what is the matter?"

Eliza sat in a chair, leaning over. She cradled her head in her hands, trying to make the room stop spinning. "I am fine, Aunt Helena. I seem to be dizzy all of a sudden."

"There, there, dear," her aunt consoled. "I will inform your uncle that we will be leaving. You rest here until I return." Her aunt patted her hand before slipping from the room.

Eliza calmed herself as her head slowly cleared. *I must say goodnight to Isabella.* She stood, waiting for the room to stop spinning. Slowly she made her way back to her friend. Miss Gibbs and Miss Pratt stood along the edge of the floor, watching the dancers.

"I am looking for Isabella," Eliza said.

"She is dancing with Mr. Phelips again," Miss Gibbs informed her. "They do make a nice couple, do they not?" Isabella's friends giggled.

Eliza's eyes scanned the dance floor and found them dancing. Isabella's eyes bright and cheerful. William looked happy, as well. Eliza's heart dropped all the way down to her gut. She hated the jittery feeling coursing through her veins, along with her skin, tingling right down through her muscles. The room grew cold. Yes, they did make a lovely couple.

"Will you inform Isabella that I had to leave?" Eliza turned and retreated.

Aunt Helena insisted she go to bed when they arrived home. Ruby helped while numbness engulfed her.

As much as she tried, sleep would not come. She played the scenario over and over in her head. How many times had she seen them whispering together? Why wouldn't Isabella want to marry William? How many times had she told Isabella that she and William were just friends? Eliza rolled over, throwing her fist into the pillow as the tears began.

Somewhere in the early morning hours she fell into a troubled sleep.

CHAPTER SEVENTEEN

*B*right sun tickled Eliza's eyelids. Groaning, she awoke from a heavy sleep. Her head pulsated while blinking back the pain the light caused. She cried again, this time from remembering the cause of her suffering.

"We let you sleep, miss, I was to check on you," Ruby spoke gently. Concern for her mistress could be heard in her voice.

"What time is it?"

"Just past noon, miss."

Eliza threw the covers over her head to block out the rays of the sun. How could it shine on a day like this?

"Your aunt is worried about you, miss. What should I tell her?"

"I am fine, Ruby. Please draw me a bath and tell my aunt I will be down shortly."

Eliza willed herself to get out of bed. It took all her strength to finish her ablutions. Ruby helped her dress, then styled her hair. The dull ache in her heart persisted. She needed to pull herself together. It was not like her to feel so down. She tried to convince herself she would get through this.

Her aunt sent up a tray, but she was not hungry. She nibbled a few bites of the toast and sipped her chocolate before giving up. It was late afternoon before Eliza worked up the courage to go downstairs. Her Aunt sat in the drawing room, working.

"Eliza, my dear." Her aunt greeted her. "I was so worried. How are you feeling this afternoon?"

Eliza tried to smile as she sat in the window seat. The warm afternoon sun streamed in through the panes, warming her bones.

"I am better this afternoon," she reassured her aunt.

"William left this morning for London. He waited, wanting to say goodbye. But after a while, I told him to go ahead. He was quite worried, as was I."

"He has left to visit Sir George." Eliza realized she could not wait around and watch William with Isabella.

"That is what he said."

"Aunt Helena, I hope you do not mind, but I really would like to go home now," Eliza informed her. "I miss my family."

Her aunt's brows knit. "Of course, you do. I will have everything arranged so that we may leave this week. Will that be acceptable?"

"Thank you, Aunt Helena." Eliza rubbed her arms as she stared out the window.

Eliza felt like a coward for returning home while William was in London. But she did not think she could watch him court Isabella, as much as she loved them both.

Eliza wrote Isabella a letter explaining her visit home. Ramsey had it delivered on the day she left.

Eliza's heart felt lighter when the carriage pulled up to the vicarage. It had been a long journey and the heaviness of her heart increased with the distance. Each mile was torture. Despite her uncle's well-sprung carriage, the road seemed to bruise her heart with each turn of the wheel. She entered her home, realizing how much she missed the place.

"Miss Eliza, it is good to have you home," the housemaid greeted her.

"Is father here?"

"Yes, miss. He is in his study."

"This is Ruby, my maid. Will you show her to my room?"

Eliza found her father bent over his desk in his office, papers strewn about.

"Father." Eliza watched as he raised his head and met her eyes.

"Lizzie, your home." He rose, embracing her in a warm comforting hug. "We did not expect you so soon."

Her eyes teared. It felt good to hear her father's voice. "I could not wait to get home and see you and Joanne. What are a few weeks?" She emitted a weak laugh.

"I am glad you are at home. I see my sister has taken good care of you." Her father gazed at her.

Eliza twirled around so he could see her. "You know your sister well, father. Aunt Helena and Uncle Donavan have been attentive indeed. They introduced me to lots of interesting people. I have learned to handle Aunt Helena's gig, which I used liberally to explore the city," Eliza explained. "I even visited the circulating library and learned about the history of Bristol."

"I am glad to hear it. It is always good for a lady to improve her mind."

"It is generous of you to say so, father. Not all parents think education is good for their daughters."

"Nonsense," the vicar replied. "I think most husbands would want an educated wife, better to teach their children."

Eliza's eyes clouded as she thought of the children she could have borne to William. She blushed at the thought. She was letting her mind run away again.

"Is Joanne home?"

"She is off visiting friends. I should think she should be home soon."

Eliza went to her room where Ruby was unpacking her small trunk. She had only planned to stay through New Year's before returning to Bristol. She would be going to Bath in March when the weather warmed. Surely Isabella would be betrothed to William by then.

CHAPTER EIGHTEEN

*A*bby called on her the next day. "I could not wait," she said as she settled into a cozy chair. "When I heard you were back from Bristol, I just had to come visit. It is good to have you home. Tell me all about your visit. William has written a few times, but he never gives me enough details. He sent word he was to visit father in London and hopes to be home soon. He has hinted at a special surprise he is bringing with him."

Eliza's heart sank at the news. He must be confident in Isabella's answer. And why shouldn't he. Any lady would be thrilled to be his wife.

"How did you find your aunt?"

"She has spoiled me terribly," Eliza admitted. "I have a whole new wardrobe for my season."

Abby's eyes widened. "I shall try to convince father to let me have a season in Bath."

Eliza brightened at the thought. "Do you really

think your father would let you come to Bath?" Having Abby with her would make it much more bearable.

"I don't see why not. Bath or London, it makes no difference to me. Father is anxious for me to find a husband." Abby giggled. "But I am not ready to settle down yet."

"If you are not careful," Eliza teased, "you will find yourself a maiden aunt."

"I have years ahead of me. It is a new age, have not you heard?" Abby scoffed.

"I am sure your father will have something to say about that," Eliza admonished.

"He said Aunt Lucy is not a good influence. He thinks she indulges me too much."

Eliza thought of Isabella's parents. "I think aunt Lucy is perfect. You know she loves you."

"Oh, yes, she does. My father complains that she loves me too much."

"I do not think you can be loved too much." Eliza felt helplessness pouring through her before she buried the emotion deep down inside to be locked away. Did she love William too much?

William returned to Bristol only to find Eliza had returned home. It had taken him some time to finish his business before he could leave London. How could he court her if she kept disappearing?

He made his way to the vicarage the morning after he returned, only waiting long enough for an acceptable time to call. The vicar welcomed him. "William, it is good to see you. When did you return? Eliza tells me you have been to London to visit your father."

"Yes, I have returned yesterday."

"How is Sir George?"

"He is well, thank you. He will be home for Christmas when parliament breaks. We look forward to your Christmas sermon. It is one of the few times of year that the family is all together," William said.

"Yes, it is good to have Lizzie home for the new year."

"Is Eliza home?" William's pulse increased at the mention of her name.

"She told me she was going for a walk after breakfast," the vicar said. "I don't believe she has returned yet."

"If you do not mind, I would like to go find her. I have something to discuss with her."

"Yes, find her if you can." The vicar excused him.

William left the vicarage on foot, suspecting Eliza was in her favorite spot. As he drew near her favorite tree, he saw her shapely form leaning against the trunk, an open book in her lap.

William smiled. It's always a book, he thought as he

approached quietly, not wanting to disturb the picture she made. How many times had he found her in this place, reading in the shade of the tree? The wintery branches were now bare, reaching for the sky.

Deep walnut brown curls blew out from underneath her hooded cape. Soft billowy eyelashes rested against her pink cheeks. Was Eliza dreaming of him? A sense of urgency drove him to his knees as he leaned in. Pulling his glove from his hand, he reached to move the curl off her cheek.

A moment of panic ran through his chest. What if Eliza did not feel for him the way he felt for her? He had given his heart, but what if she rejected it? Isabella insisted she wouldn't.

Lightly, he fingered the loose tendril of hair as her eyes fluttered open and focused on his face.

"William! You're home?"

He reached out, lacing her fingers with his own. They warmed at her touch.

Eliza's stomach flipped as she gazed into William's smiling eyes. He shifted his weight and settled down next to her.

"Your father told me you had gone for a walk. I guessed you would be here."

"Have you returned from London, then? Did you finish your business?" Eliza asked in a soft voice.

"Yes, I needed my father's advice and then I went back to Bristol to finish some business before coming home. You were gone. I thought you would be there when I returned."

Fear twisted around her heart. She stood and began to walk. William followed.

"I have good news, Eliza. I could not wait to tell you. That is why I have come so early." He reached over and touched her arm, bringing her to a halt.

She would be brave. After all, she loved William, and Isabella was her friend. "I am happy for you, William, and Isabella as well. I am sure you will both be very happy. Has she returned with you?" She pulled away, keeping her eyes on the ground.

"Isabella?" His voice sounded confused.

Eliza looked up.

"You were courting Isabella, were you not? That was your business in Bristol. I know you spoke with her father." Eliza held her breath, waiting for confirmation. Had he asked for her hand?

"Eliza," William reached for her. Taking both her arms, he turned her towards him. His jaw clenched as his eyes narrowed. "I have not been courting Isabella," he stated firmly. "I have been *courting you*!"

If he had told her she had two heads, she would not have been more astonished. "Me? You have been courting me? But you said we were only friends."

Her wide eyes searched his. He groaned as he raked

his hand through his hair. "Why do you think I have been spending so much time with you?"

She shook her head at a loss for words. "Because we are friends?"

He pulled at his hair as he paced in front of her.

"Mrs. Dalton said..." He turned to stare. "You were speaking with her husband. I thought you were asking for Isabella's hand."

He deflated. "Mrs. Dalton did have hopes in that direction but Isabella knew it was you I loved."

"You love me?"

William reached for her, sweeping her into the circle of his arms, embracing her tight, his lips met hers urgently, willing her to believe him. Then softened as she responded. He lifted his head, leaving her without breath. "Is this what friends do?" he rasped.

Her heart raced as fear melted away replaced by something sweet and wonderful. *He loves me.* Smiling, she twined her fingers around his neck pulling him into another embrace meeting his lips again. No, this didn't feel like friendship, but something much more.

William finally pulled away giving her a chance to breathe. Clasping her hands in his, he leaned his forehead against hers. "I love you, Eliza," he declared softly. "I want you to be my wife."

Her heart did somersaults at his words. "Oh, William, yes, yes, I want that too." A knot rose in her throat as she melted back into his caress.

"Come, I think we should talk to your father."

William pulled her toward the vicarage as he cradled her by his side. William let go of her hand as they neared the vicarage. What would her father say? She felt dazed, still processing that William loved her.

They found him in his study, looking up as they entered. "I see you have found Eliza."

"Sir," William responded, "could I have a word with you? Alone. Now?"

Her father adjusted his spectacles, a question in his eyes. "Yes. Lizzie, would you excuse us?" Eliza blinked at her father then focused her gaze on William. Her heart filled with happiness as she gently closed the door behind her. She retreated to the drawing-room and waited nervously pacing the room. Her father would agree, he had to.

CHAPTER NINETEEN

The longer William looked at the vicar, the more his nerves increased. In all his plans, he had not thought about talking to Eliza's father. William's insides knotted as he stood twisting his hands behind his back.

"Come, William," the vicar stated. "Out with it."

"Well sir, I love your daughter. Eliza and I would like your permission to marry."

The vicar's eyes grew wide as his mouth dropped open. He hesitated before standing. "I must say this is a surprise. How does my daughter feel?"

"She has agreed, with your permission, sir," William informed him. "We have been courting while in Bristol, sir."

Well — he had been *trying* to court Eliza. It had apparently been one-sided. Thank heavens he had straightened that out. Where had she ever gotten the idea that he was courting Isabella?

The vicar was shaking his hand enthusiastically. "Of course, you have my blessing William. I will be glad to welcome you to the family. Have you spoken to your father about this?"

"I have, sir," William replied. "I spoke with him while in London, and he is very pleased with my choice and gives me his blessing."

The vicar chuckled as they left the study and joined Eliza.

"Father," Eliza exclaimed concerned, then relief when she saw his arm on William's shoulder.

"My dear, I am greatly surprised, but I have given my blessing for you to marry William."

William watched Eliza step into her father's arms, giving him a soft embrace. "Thank you, Father, I am so happy."

"What about me?" William teased.

With a giggle, Eliza stepped toward him, molding herself into his arms. He squeezed her close, resting his chin on her head. The floral scent of her hair calming him.

"Well," the vicar interrupted, "I suppose you would like the banns read this Sunday?"

William looked into Eliza's eyes. She nodded her consent. "Yes, sir, we would. I was thinking of a wedding during the new year. My father will be here, so the family will be together."

Eliza's eyes pooled as she agreed. "William, that will be so nice having the whole family together. And, of course, we will invite my uncle and aunt as well as Isabella." Her eyes clouded. "Do you think her family will allow her to come?"

"All you can do is send an invitation," William gave her a slight squeeze. "Now you are all invited to dinner tomorrow where we will announce the good news to my family."

William spent half an hour at the vicarage discussing their plans before riding home a happy man.

William's family gathered along with Eliza's at Montacute under the guise of a welcome home dinner. They had of course, invited Lord and Lady Malmesbury, for they were considered family.

Eliza had told her sister last night, of course, and Joanne was so happy for her. Eliza's eyes sparkled as William stood, tapping the side of his glass. He cleared his throat. All eyes turned at the sound.

"I would like to thank you for coming out to our family celebration as we come to the end of this year and welcome Eliza home." The room erupted in a round of applause and exuberant cheers. Eliza blushed, a warm feeling spreading through her. William raised his arms quieting the crowd.

"I would like to make a toast," Williams began. "To

Eliza, who has consented to be my wife." He nodded towards her and raised his glass.

A moment of stunned silence followed, then a squeal sounded as Abby jumped up and ran to Eliza smothering her in a hug. "You are going to be my sister." She cried as laughter erupted around them.

"Abby, let Eliza have some air," Aunt Lucy admonished her niece.

A few moments elapsed before the room settled. William invited everyone to the parlor where the gentlemen could enjoy some brandy while the women visited. Abby and Susan linked arms, flanking Eliza as they followed the gentlemen.

"You must tell us all about your courtship," Abby gushed as they settled in a corner, each taking a seat beside her.

Abby's Aunt Lucy and the dowager countess seated themselves nearby, and Joanne squeezed beside her. Embarrassed, Eliza did not know what to say. Dare she admit she had not realized William had been courting her?

She glanced across the room where William and his friends were talking, enjoying their drinks. William caught her eye, and his mouth quirked with humor. She flushed, turning her attention back to the women. Abby's bright eyes shined. She had been watching her?

"What?" Eliza inquired.

"I can't believe you and my brother are in love."

"Abby, when will you learn to tame your tongue?" Aunt Lucy scolded her.

"I think it is wonderful. We are so happy for you both." Susan squeezed Eliza's hand.

"You must let us help you plan the wedding," Abby exclaimed, once again excited.

"Oh." Eliza had not thought that far ahead. "Well, my Aunt Helena will come and she can be a force."

"That is fine, Eliza. We would not get in your aunt's way, but we would love to give you our support." Aunt Lucy reassured her.

"That would be most generous of you."

"Now, Eliza, you must call me Aunt Lucy. You are to be family soon."

"And we will be here as well," Susan and the dowager countess agreed.

"If it was your aunt that dressed you Eliza, she has excellent taste." The dowager countess smiled.

"Thank you, my lady, I think you and my aunt will get along."

Eliza thought the evening went well as she rode home with her father and Joanne.

"Father, I must write to Aunt Helena tomorrow. She will want to know the good news as she liked William very much."

"That will be good Lizzie, but I fear she will fly down here and take over everything."

Eliza chuckled. "Yes, Father, she will."

CHAPTER TWENTY

*E*liza removed her garden gloves. A chilly wind blew in the waning afternoon as she prepared the herb pots for winter. Brushing a wisp of hair from her eyes, she peered around the cold room and removed her apron before entering the house.

"Lizzie, Father, Aunt Helena has arrived," Joanne announced excitedly.

"So, she has," the vicar replied, as Aunt Helena swept into the entrance hall. Her father planted a kiss on his sister's cheek.

"Aunt Helena," Eliza greeted, dusting off her skirt in time to give her aunt a welcoming hug. Luggage was already being unloaded behind her.

"I have brought the rest of your dresses, dear. I shall stay for tea, and then I am off to Montacute where William's Aunt Lucy has invited me to stay."

Her aunt took her arm, and they went into the

drawing-room. "I think this will be a good arrangement as we plan the wedding. How is your William?"

Eliza broke into a wide-open smile. "He has been very attentive. I confess I am happy to turn the details of this wedding over to you. William and I have seen each other every day, and it has been delightful getting to know him in a different way."

Aunt Helena chuckled knowingly. "You enjoy being betrothed?"

"Very much," Eliza replied. Her face clouded over for a moment. "Though I must confess, I am apprehensive of my duties once we are married."

"You are a smart girl,besides you will have a housekeeper," Aunt Helena reminded her. "Lucy is in charge until William inherits. You have plenty of time. William tells me his aunt is very accommodating."

Eliza held the teacup, careful not to spill the hot liquid as she finished pouring. She had not thought about Aunt Lucy and her responsibilities. Eliza handed the delicate porcelain cup to her aunt. "William's Aunt Lucy adores him and Abby, his sister," Eliza replied. She poured another cup of tea for her sister Joanne. "I am relieved William's aunt will be with us." Eliza relaxed in her chair, sipping the warm liquid.

Aunt Helena gave them all a quick goodbye and left the vicarage as quickly as she had swooped in.

With the efficiency of three mature ladies and time, the day of Eliza's wedding was here. She was reassured in the knowledge that after this day, she and William would be bound together for the rest of their lives.

Those beloved three ladies, Aunt Lucy, Aunt Helena, and the dowager countess, helped Eliza dress for her special day. She had chosen a simple gown of pale blue, trimmed with lace along the neck and sleeves, with a soft white satin ribbon falling just below the bust. She wrapped herself in a fur-lined cloak to protect against the chilly wind. Her friends and sister escorted her.

Her stomach did a little jump as she caught sight of William waiting, with his friends, Lord Malmesbury and Captain Rutley. His father, Sir George, sat with Aunt Lucy, her uncle, and aunt, along with the dowager countess. Everyone she loved was present. It could not be more perfect.

William's brilliant blue eyes followed her movements until she reached his side. Standing before her father, they completed their vows, each agreeing to love, honor, and obey. Placing the ring on her finger, he bent and gently brushed his lips to hers, sealing their commitment with a kiss.

The register had been signed; it was official. William took her hand as they moved towards the chapel doors.

Drawing her close, he whispered, tickling her ear, "I

have brought your surprise, my gift to you. I hope you like it."

They emerged into a cloudy day. Soft flakes had begun to fall, wetting her cheeks. Neighbors and villagers had gathered to cheer and welcome the new couple. A liveried carriage was waiting to take them to Montacute where food would be served to all who came, an afternoon of celebrating a new life together.

Eliza's eyes popped as she gazed at the little figure holding the carriage door, his perfect white teeth gleaming in his little brown face from ear to ear.

"Sam," Eliza exclaimed, turning her wet eyes to William. "You brought Sam?"

"Miss Eliza," little Sam exclaimed as they neared the carriage. "Master William is teaching me to drive, and I get to attend the horses."

William reached out and ruffled Sam's head. "Only after you finish your schooling."

"Yes, Master William." Sam turned and scrambled up to sit next to the driver.

William closed the door, and the carriage moved off. He pulled Eliza toward him, tucking her by his side. "Do you like your gift?"

"Oh, William." Her eyes shined. "It's perfect, but how did you manage to bring Sam here?"

"Isabella helped. Her father introduced me to Sam's owner. It appears he was glad to be rid of him. Sam is constantly running off. He is a curious little boy, but bright."

176 of KAREN LYNNE

"Isabella," Eliza breathed. "Is that why the two of you appeared so intimate?"

William laughed out loud. "Yes, and her parents hoped we would be married. That's why she was given so much freedom in our company."

William squeezed her hand. "I'm sorry she wasn't able to come to our wedding."

Eliza gazed into his eyes, and she reached her hand and stroked his cheek. "Thank you," she whispered.

He'd given her so much and now Sam was free. Free to learn and frolic as a child should. She would write Isabella and thank her.

William grasped her hand and turned it over. He placed a kiss on her palm, sending a thrill all the way down to her toes where it bounced and spun its way into her heart.

Authors Notes

Montacute House was built in 1588 by Sir Edward Phelips following a successful career as a lawyer. He served as master of the roles until his death in 1614. Montacute was built as a summer home for his family, and on his death, his son Sir Robert Phelips inherited the estate. Montacute House was sold to Ernest cook in 1931 who presented to the society for the Protection of Ancient Buildings and was then passed to the National Trust.

Films that used Montacute House in several scenes include the 1995 film version of Sense and Sensibility. 2004 The Libertine. 2014 for Wolf Hall.

Bristol and Liverpool became centers of the Triangular Trade. On the first side of the slavery triangle, manufactured goods were shipped to West Africa and exchanged for Africans; the enslaved captives were transported across the Atlantic to the Americas in the Middle Passage under brutal conditions. On the third side of the triangle, plantation goods such as sugar, tobacco, rum, rice, cotton and a few slaves (sold to the aristocracy as house servants) returned across the Atlantic. (Information from USI website)

Asphaltum, an old English term for asphalt, was mixed with aggregate and patented as a road base in 1838. It was used to make roads in Bristol. I have used this in my book, knowing it is twenty years beyond the novels period. I took several author privileges in this work of fiction.

*L*ady Abigale was used to getting her way, but it was nearing the end of her third Season in London. Her father, Sir George, was concerned for her and felt she should have been married by now. It wasn't for lack of suitors that Abby hadn't "stuck," as they say. She had turned down two young men who had wished to propose already this Season. A fact she kept to herself.

Abby threw her bonnet on the side table and entered the parlor of her father's London townhome. A spring shower hung wet in the air, cutting short her morning ride in the park. It was just as well she was growing tired of the daily visits from suitors who left her feeling weary.

If her father had just let her go to Bath for the Season. She had been writing to her friend Isabella, who lived in Bristol and enjoyed the Bath Season. She had hoped to enjoy the smaller community with Isabella, where she could develop more intimate friendships.

Aunt Lucy looked up from her stitching when Abby entered the room. Abby dropped onto the settee next to her aunt, brushing a damp curl out of her face. Aunt Lucy, her father's sister, had been her chaperone and companion ever since her mother died. She was a most affectionate, indulgent aunt; doting and loving, although she too was beginning to lose patience with her.

"Abby, dear, you're damp. Is that why you're back so soon?"

"I'm afraid it began to drizzle just as we entered the park. Thank heavens I had my parasol. I think my dress can be dried without any damage." Abby attempted to brush the drops from her skirt before she gave up. Betsy, her maid, would bring the dress back to life. It really was fortuitous that they had been caught in the shower. Her companion, though sweet, in a boyish, innocent way, was dull and stirred no passion as a young lady would hope.

"I think you ordered that rain on purpose, Abby, just to get out from riding with your new beau."

Her brother, William, startled her. She hadn't seen him sitting in the corner, his face buried in the London Post. He lowered the paper just enough to stare at her, shaking his head.

Abby's eyes drilled into his. "Mr. Wyler is not my beau."

"Well, he could be if you would give him a chance."

William continued to stare at his sister, giving her a knowing look.

"Mr. Wyler does not stir my emotions."

"Stir your emotions?" Her brother laughed, "Abby, everybody stirs your emotions. You're the most excitable female I've ever come across. If you keep this up, I wager you'll be a spinster by next Season just like your friend, Miss Underwood."

"Josephine is not a spinster; she's an independent woman."

"An independent spinster, no doubt," William egged her on. "Mark my word, Abby. If you keep this up, in the next year or two, gentlemen will begin to avoid you."

Abby clutched the arms of the chair as she maintained her temper. "You will see, William. I will take that wager and prove to you that I am capable of finding a husband. A husband that will suit *me,* not you or Father." She stood, flouncing out of the room, her damp skirts sticking to her legs. She could hear her aunt reprimanding William as she made her escape.

"You know you will push her into doing something rash by your teasing, William."

Abby made her way to her bedchamber where Betsy helped her out of her damp clothing. A hot bath would set her to rights. How dare her brother insinuate that she was changeable. She deserved a husband whom she had passion for. Didn't she?

William had found his love two Seasons back. Her

dear friend, Eliza, and he had fallen in love and married, and she knew they loved each other deeply. She was beginning to think that it was not possible for her to find love.

The gentlemen she had met these past few Seasons were either too old or too young, tied to their mothers, and unable to think for themselves. They sparked no emotion, Abby wanted to feel something for her husband. So far, her father hadn't pushed her to marry anyone, but she didn't know how long his patience would hold.

Abby spent the morning riding in Hyde Park with Miss Josephine Underwood, taking advantage of the cool morning. They managed their horses along the serpentine, avoiding the footpaths. A groom followed at a discreet distance at the insistence of her father.

It was a clear day, and the rain had abated, making the ride enjoyable. She enjoyed her time with Miss Underwood. Josephine was a self-proclaimed spinster at the ripe old age of twenty-eight. Her parents had died and left her enough money to be independent.

Abby deemed herself fortunate Josephine allowed her to be friends and to call her by her given name. Miss Underwood didn't suffer the fair sex's company often, preferring more mature acquaintances. She was taller than average, and her sharp eyes looking down her straight nose could quell any silly miss in an instant. Josephine was going to Bath for the summer and had invited Abby to come as her guest.

"I have found a house in Bath." Josephine shifted the reins and turned her mount, avoiding the children who ran through the grass as their nannies gossiped amongst themselves, turning their heads every so often to check on their charges.

"So soon?" Abby asked in surprise for Josephine had just decided to go to the country a couple of weeks past.

"Yes, I was fortunate a family left suddenly without giving notice, and my man snapped it up. It's a very upscale address in the Royal Crescent, number 20. Have you talked to your father about staying with me this summer?"

Abby shook her head. "I have been waiting for the right moment. This has to be handled delicately. He is still peeved at me for discouraging Mr. Thomas."

Josephine laughed. "I understand, and the invitation stands. I will be leaving at the end of the week before the summer heat sets in. Send me word of your decision, but I warn you, I keep myself busy with charitable work, and it can be quite dull."

"It will be a change from the parties that fill our days in London," Abby complained. "But I am sure I shall find a way to get to Bath."

Abby waved goodbye as she and Josephine emerged from the park gate and promised to send word. Abby headed towards her father's townhouse still early as hawkers readied their carts, preparing to sell for the day. Nannies were already bringing their charges for a romp in the park before the crowds of ladies and gentlemen took the daily strolls.

A groom took Abby's mount and she entered the front door. She could hear her father in the breakfast parlor with her Aunt Lucy. Climbing the stairs to her room for a quick freshening up before she joined them deciding this morning was as good a time as any to broach the subject. She knew her father loved her, but could be stern. Taking a deep breath, running her hands down the front of her skirt, she entered the breakfast room.

"Abby, dear," her aunt's eyes brightened, "did you have a good ride?"

"Oh, I did. It was lovely." Abby sat and placed a napkin in her lap. She reached for a triangle of toast and buttered it. A footman poured her a cup of tea while she helped herself to a boiled egg and began to crack it, avoiding her father's eyes. Keeping her voice light, she said before biting into her toast, "Miss Underwood has invited me to stay with her in Bath this summer."

"Oh." Her Aunt Lucy looked up, blinking.

"Bath, why would you want to go to Bath? We've been over this." Her father laid his paper down on the table, raising his eyes to her. "You haven't managed to catch a husband here in London with thousands of people. Why would Bath be any different?"

Abby opened her mouth to respond when her aunt coughed. "Abby, why don't you let your father and I talk about this?" She gave her a knowing look, signaling Abby was dismissed.

Abby thought it a good idea. Finishing her egg, she stuffed the last bite of toast in her mouth, wiped her hands, and stood. Giving her aunt a nod, she quickly left the room, closing the door behind her leaving just a crack. What was Aunt Lucy up to? She leaned her ear towards the door. Would her aunt support her with this invitation?

"Lucy, what was that about?" Her father huffed.

"George, why do you insist on provoking your daughter so? I see no reason why Abby can't go and visit her friend in Bath this summer. You won't even be home most of the summer."

"William and Eliza are taking good care of the estate. Why should I drag myself back to the country?" Sir George defended himself.

"Exactly, how do you think Abby feels? Both Susan and Eliza, her friends, are married now. She has nobody else close to her age. It would do her good to go to Bath. If you're worried about her, I will contact Eliza's aunt, Mrs. Notley, in Bristol. I hear she's taken her niece to Bath for the Season."

"You won't be going with her?" Father's voice became alarmed.

"Abby will reach her majority this summer. I feel no need to go with her to Bath. There will be plenty of escorts, and she will have her maid with her. Betsy is a sensible girl."

Abby heard a cough. She turned her head to see the butler staring at her a frown on his face. She lifted her finger to her lips and bent closer to the opening. The butler raised his eyes to the ceiling and continued down the hall.

She couldn't believe Aunt Lucy was championing her cause. Her heart sped up in anticipation of going to Bath, *finally*.

"What do we know about this Miss Underwood?" her father continued. "I'm concerned that she might be a bad influence on Abby."

"You mean to become a spinster, like myself." Aunt Lucy had raised her voice. It carried a slight edge.

"Lucy, I didn't mean…" Her father's voice softened.

"Never you mind. If you must know, Mr. Albert is spending time with me. Now that Abby is reaching her majority, I would like to take some time for myself."

"It's not nice to eavesdrop." A soft breath blew against her ear. Jumping back, her hand flew to her chest. William stood behind her a stern looks on his face as he tapped his foot.

"When it concerns me, it is," she threw back at him, tossing her head.

He reached for her elbow and pulled her forward. "Come, Abby, walk me to the door."

A footman was loading bags onto the back of William's curricle. "You're leaving?"

"Yes, my business is done here, and I'd like to get back to my wife. Eliza has been managing the estate for a month now. It's time I returned to her and my boy."

Abby kicked her toe against the stones as William checked his horses. "William, did you know Mr. Albert was spending time with Aunt Lucy?"

"He is? Well, good for them." William turned to adjust his luggage.

Frustrated Abby slapped her hand against her skirt. "Is that all you have to say?" What if Aunt Lucy leaves us?

He turned to look at her. "I think it's time Aunt Lucy found a little companionship of her own. She's been taking care of us for a long time. You should worry about our wager," he advised. "I shall be thinking of what you will owe me when you lose our wager." He leaned down and tweaked her cheek. Abby swatted at his hand.

"You know I like a challenge, William, so don't think you'll win this one." She watched him climb into his curricle. He tipped his hat as he moved into the street. Shaking her head, she entered the house again. Knowing when to leave the fight to someone else, Abby retired to her room and left Aunt Lucy to convince her father.

Abby had not thought to go to Bath without the companionship of her aunt. She had enjoyed the affection and kindness of her company for the past sixteen years. Her mother died when Abby was at a tender age. The only motherly affection she remembered had come from her aunt.

Not being a selfish creature, Abby was happy her aunt might find a place of her own. Mr. Albert was a man of exceptionally good character, good fortune, and a sensible age for aunt Lucy. They would get on well together.

CHAPTER TWO

*S*ir Andrew Pulteney, the fifth Baronet of Bath, was ready to go home to his Bathwick estate. It had been a trying session. They had been unable to get a bill, to clarify the Slave Trade Act of 1807, which Sir George Phelips had brought forward through the House of Commons for legislation. The bill had been bouncing around the house for the last several years. It seemed no one wanted to commit, and so the debates continued.

Andrew entered White's Club on 37 James Street, a copy of the Edinburgh tucked under his arm. He found members of Parliament discussing the bills that were currently before the House.

Sir George welcomed him to a seat. "Sir Andrew, we were just discussing that if Jenkinson would call a vote, we might get the Slave Trade Act expanded throughout the British Empire."

Andrew sat, putting his paper aside. "You may try, Sir George, but I believe we don't have enough votes yet. We've been debating this for the last two sessions."

"You're probably right." Sir George's brow wrinkled. "We only have a month left before we break. I guess it's too much to hope for a positive conclusion."

"Yes, I agree so I've decided to head home. I haven't seen my son for a while." Andrew pushed the paper toward Sir George. "Did you hear the Pentrich rising has been stopped? They hung the ringleaders at the Derby ghoul."

Sir George reached for the paper, shaking his head. "The Luddites broke up lace-making machines in Loughborough in February. I don't agree with their tactics, but I understand the recession has hit the working class hard."

"I believe it will take time. The war has only ended these past two years, it's painful to accept change, especially when it affects your livelihood." Sir Andrew replied.

"You reside in Bath, do you not?" Sir George asked.

"I do, in the parish of Bathwick where I have a large estate."

Sir George sat and pondered as if something heavy weighed on his mind. "My daughter, Lady Abigale, is visiting Bath this summer with a friend, Miss Underwood. She will be leaving within the week. My sister believes it will be good for her, but I have my concerns."

Andrew recalled the young miss he'd seen several Seasons ago. Like many of the young debutantes, he tended to avoid them. "We have many visitors during the summer. They take the waters and avoid the hot London summer."

"Yes. My sister has given me all the arguments, but I would feel reassured. If you could check on her, nothing formal . . . Just if you happen to see her in society, it will put my mind at ease as she is reaching her majority this summer."

While Andrew certainly didn't want to play nursemaid, he tried to remember what the lady looked like. Blonde, pretty face, full of giggles like the rest of her kind. He should make an excuse, but he respected Sir George, and as a father, he could sympathize with his concern. He nodded as he found himself agreeing. "Give me her address, and I will see what I can do."

He would make a courtesy call to the girl and set Sir George's mind at ease. Then it would be done, and he could turn to his duties at home. He hadn't remarried after his wife died shortly after the birth of their son. She was docile and met his needs. It hadn't been a love match, but he did not need to love his wife. It was less complicated that way.

He hadn't given much thought to it lately, but it was probably time to think of remarrying for the sake of his son. A mature lady would be best, someone who didn't expect anything from him, but someone who could guide his young son until he was old enough to be sent

to school. Then his wife could do as she pleased. He had
plenty of money, that wasn't a problem as long as his
wife didn't interfere with his comfortable life.

Sir George was true to his word and sent the address
of where his daughter would be staying, along with the
direction of Mrs. Notley of Bristol, who could be
notified if need be.

Miss Underwood, 20 Royal Crescent Bath. The
residence was in a good part of town, which gave him
pause. He was not about to get caught up in Bath society
and hoped he would not regret helping Sir George.

Abby woke up to sunshine and a happy countenance.
Aunt Lucy had somehow convinced her father to let her
spend the summer in Bath. Miss Josephine Underwood
had left three days before and promised to have the
house set up by the time Abby arrived.

Arrangements had been made for her to travel with
Mrs. Packett and her two daughters. Not the best
traveling with the Packett sisters for they tended to
quarrel amongst themselves. It could be tedious to be
trapped in a coach together. But she wouldn't complain.
Surely, she could endure two days of travel when the
reward was a summer in Bath.

Betsy had finished her packing, and they were to
leave on the morning coach. Aunt Lucy had given her
strict instructions and reminded her to behave like a

lady. She promised she would come for a visit later in the summer. Mrs. Notley of Bristol had been informed, and Abby could expect an invitation.

Mrs. Packett and her daughters met Abby at the station and made their greetings. "Lady Abigale, it was good of your father to allow us to accompany you as far as Bath."

"Oh no, Mrs. Packett, I am most grateful for you to escort me." Abby gave her a slight nod and a pretty smile.

The sisters giggled, and Miss Millicent nudged her sister. Lady Abigale, I have brought a guide book and look forward to pointing out the interesting historical sights."

Abby smiled. "As we are going to be together for the next two days, please call me Abby."

"Oh, lovely, and you may call me Liz, and my sister is called Milly by her friends."

Liz gave Abby a wide smile before heading to their coach where the luggage and trunks had been loaded. No sooner had they left and turned towards the Tyburn Turnpike when Liz, who sat by a window, began to watch the scenery, keeping her place in her book. An hour later they passed through the village of Southhall.

"Southhall supports a weekly market on Thursdays where they sell cattle, which are the best in Middlesex, except those held in Smithfield," Liz informed them.

"Cattle, *cattle*! What do we care about cattle?" Milly screeched.

"Cattle are vital, especially to Southhall," her sister argued.

Their mother, Mrs. Packett, had dozed off soon after they left London. Abby was amazed that she could sleep through all the bumping and swaying of the coach and the constant arguments of her daughters.

Abby turned to the window, watching the scenery go by. A small church made of flint and brick came into view it was a neat structure with a tower at its west end. It looked to have been built hundreds of years before but must have been well cared for by the villagers. Memories of the vicarage back home and its chapel came to mind. The church of Saint Catherine, it had been built in the twelfth century and updated through the centuries. Her ancestors were buried in the adjourning cemetery.

The coach stopped, bringing her out of her thoughts. She welcomed the rest and a short break. Betsy followed Abby through the inn to a room set up for female travelers. She freshened up, then followed her nose; the smell of fresh pastries wafted through the air. She bought two buns with ham and cheese and five apple tarts that were still warm from the oven to eat on the trip.

The crunch of wheels could be heard on the cobblestones. The door swung open, and a tall man in a dark cloak pushed his way through brushing past Abby, he turned, his sharp eyes gazing down at her face before moving past. Abby's skin tingled, she took notice of his commanding manner. Was he someone important?

She moved outside where a black lacquered coach rounded the corner of the inn. Walking to the edge of the building, she peered in awe as it was an exceptionally built carriage with a gold and red B monogrammed on the door. Four brilliant black horses pulled the sleek vehicle. Surely it was designed for speed Abby thought.

Her coach driver signaled their departure, and she hurried to board. Abby shared her meal with Betsy and wiped her hands on the napkin before pulling out an apple tart and handing one to each of the occupants.

"Thank you, Lady Abigale, for your consideration," Mrs. Packett acknowledged as she took one of the apple tarts. Her daughters parroted their mothers' thanks before hastily devouring the treat.

Abby took a taste of the apple tart and closed her eyes, slowly savouring each bite. It reminded her of home. Mrs. Baxter made the best pastries. She was the housekeeper and cook at Fyne Court, Lady Susan's childhood home. Mrs. Baxter was a jolly person who enjoyed teaching Abby to make apple tarts. "It's a way to a man's heart," she would say. "Even the finest lady should be able to cook a few treats." She didn't mind Abby spending time in the kitchen with her. It was an activity she would never have been allowed to do at her father's home at Montacute. Their cook was persnickety about his kitchen.

Abby tried to rest, but the noise the sisters were making prevented any meaningful sleep. When the coach pulled into the inn for the night, Abby's nerves were stretched to their limits, although Betsy seemed to be in good spirits. How was she going to make it through another day? The Old Crown Coaching Inn, the sign read. She needed some food and a respite from the constant chatter of the Packett girls.

They retired to their rooms after dining. Abby and Betsy were led to a small room facing the front of the inn while Mrs. Packett and her daughters slept in the room at the back.

Restless, Abby soon slipped out with Betsy for a short walk under the full moon when the jingle of harnesses brought her attention to the same sleek black coach she had seen earlier pull into the inn. Its impressive owner stepped out and mumbled directions to the grooms before going into the Old Crown. Abby nudged her maid, "Betsy, go find who owns the coach and where they are bound."

Betsy scampered off to talk to the grooms appearing back shortly, she informed her mistress, "Tis Sir Andrew Pulteney, the fifth Baronet of Bath. His man says he's headed home to Bath this very evening. They're only stopping for a few hours to rest the horses. With the light of the full moon, he bragged they should make it by dawn."

Abby could believe it with those prime horses. Her mind formed an idea as she and her maid walked to and fro in front of the inn, careful to stay in the light of the lamps. "Betsy, how would you like to make it to Bath this night and not have to listen to the Packett sisters?"

"Would be a blessing to my ears, my lady," Betsy said, "but what have you planned?"

They returned to their room as Abby explained to Betsy what they needed to do. They had a servant carefully bring their luggage back down and set it on the corner of the building so as not to be seen through the windows.

Abby had removed a black cloak from her trunk and wrapped it around her. Pulling the hood over her hair, she sat down and waited for Sir Andrew to finished his business, then Betsy went into action.

"Please, sir." A petite girl looked up at Andrew as he was paying the innkeeper. He looked into her eyes and listened as she continued. "Your man tells us you are headed to Bath this evening."

"Yes," Andrew answered, keeping his voice firm. He looked at her with suspicion.

"My mistress, an elderly widow, is on her way to Bath. She has received news from her son that her grandson is very sick and wishes to see her for fear he will die. She fears if she waits for the morning coach, she may not be there on time. We would ask for a small favor. If you could give us a ride, it would greatly be appreciated."

Andrew could feel his insides tightening. He preferred his solitude. "Where is your mistress?"

"She is just outside, sir, waiting with her luggage."

Andrew stepped to the door and noticed a dark figure wrapped in a cloak sitting on a trunk of excellent quality.

"You look to be of quality, sir, and we feel with your escort, we would be safely delivered to Bath by morning." The young miss gave him a pleading look.

As Andrew contemplated the situation, compassion took over, and he walked towards the widow.

"Sir." The miss stopped him. "She prefers her solitude and is very tired from this day's journey. We won't be any trouble. If you would just say yay or nay, that will do."

Andrew could feel his ire rising. He wanted this trip to be done with and hated unnecessary complications. His life ran smoothly, and that was how he liked it, but he could not just leave a widow sitting alone in the dark when he had the means to help.

"Very well. I'll have my man load your luggage, and you may help your mistress into the coach."

"Oh, thank you, sir." The miss responded excitedly. "I shall inform my mistress."

~

Abby couldn't believe their luck as she slowly ascended the steps, trying to appear as feeble as possible. She kept her head ducked under her hood while she seated herself in the far corner, tucking her cloak further around her.

Betsy sat next to her as they listened to Sir Andrew shout orders to his men. He was soon sitting opposite them in the coach. He tapped his cane up on the roof. The coach lurched forward, and they were on their way into the darkness.

Abby laid her head against the side of the carriage and feigned sleep, willing him not to speak to her. She must have dozed off for soon Betsy was giving her a nudge, and she opened her eyes. She could just see the light of dawn coming through the carriage window.

"If you would give me your address, we can set you down at your door," Sir Andrew offered.

"Oh, we have given our address to your man," Betsy spoke up.

Abby stole a glance from under her hood watching as Sir Andrew talked to Betsy. He had a look of confusion as if he wanted to say something. But then his face cleared and he held his tongue. His well-dressed attire of dark colors was not of the latest fashion but of good quality. He'd been leafing through a stack of papers by his side, reading as the light of morning came through the windows.

Abby looked up at the impressive façade, and her heart leaped as the coach stopped in front of 20 Royal Crescent. A smile appeared on her lips as she lowered the hood of her cloak. Finally, she made it safely to Bath.

Sir Andrew's men were efficient. As soon as the coach stopped, the door was opened, and the step lowered. The lady's companion descended with Andrew following. The men were already unloading the luggage and carrying them to the door of number 20 Royal Crescent. His brows knit together as he realized the address was the same given to him by Sir George.

He looked into the carriage while the matron looked out the window. She lowered the hood of her cape, and golden curls fell across her shoulders, turning her smiling face toward him. Crystal blue eyes met his in the early light of dawn. Lady Abigale's familiar face had matured into a distinctive beauty. A stirring deep inside began to rise, but before he could utter a word, she moved towards him, stepping out of the carriage.

"Sir Andrew, we are so grateful for delivering us safely to Bath. I hope we can repay you for your kindness." Her clear melodic voice resonated through him.

She was ascending the steps of the home before he could respond. A butler opened the door, his clear voice could be heard in the street. "Lady Phelips, we have been expecting you." Lady Abigale stepped through the door and was gone.

Andrew continued to stare at the door of number twenty. She knew his name; he thought as he slowly climbed into his carriage and sank into the seat. The little minx—, he'd been duped. What had he gotten himself into?

Read more on Amazon…

ABOUT THE AUTHOR

As Karen Lynne, I write sweet historical romances, regency period being my favorite.

I love history and have been reading hundreds of romances since high school. Timeless authors where the hero and heroine are virtuous with sweet happy endings.

When I am not writing, I enjoy time with my sweetheart, my children and grandchildren and long lunches with my two reading buddies. You know who you are.

Gardening vegetables and fruits in my garden and living in our 1863 stone cottage in the Rocky Mountains.

Life is good!

Made in United States
Orlando, FL
24 June 2022

19117298R00126